Frank Moore

Rebel Rhymes and Rhapsodies

Frank Moore

Rebel Rhymes and Rhapsodies

ISBN/EAN: 9783744793445

Printed in Europe, USA, Canada, Australia, Japan

Cover: Foto ©Andreas Hilbeck / pixelio.de

More available books at **www.hansebooks.com**

REBEL RHYMES AND RHAPSODIES

COLLECTED AND EDITED BY

FRANK MOORE

NEW YORK

GEORGE P. PUTNAM

1864

RIVERSIDE, CAMBRIDGE:

STEREOTYPED AND PRINTED BY H. O. HOUGHTON AND COMPANY.

NOTE.

IN the preparation of this volume, it has been the purpose of the Editor to present as full a selection of the Songs and Ballads of the Southern people as will illustrate the spirit which actuates them in their Rebellion against the Government and Laws of the United States. Most of the pieces have been published in the magazines and periodical literature of the South, while many are copies of ballad-sheets and songs circulated in the Rebel armies, and which have come into the possession of the forces of the Union in their various marches and advances during the present conflict.

F. M.

New York, March, 1864.

CONTENTS.

		PAGE
A Poem for the Times........*John R. Thompson*....		1
Hurrying On...............*Anonymous*..........		4
A Southern Song.............*L. M.*.............		6
Southern War-Cry..........*Anonymous*..........		8
The Star of the West........*Anonymous*..........		9
Farewell to Brother Jonathan..*Caroline*............		10
Call all! Call all!...........*"Georgia"*		13
What the South Winds Say...*Anonymous*..........		14
The Ordered Away...........*Mrs. J. J. Jacobus*....		16
The Martyr of Alexandria.....*J. W. S.*............		19
Southrons, hear your Country call you.................*Albert Pike*..........		20
The Right above the Wrong ..*John W. Overall*......		23
The Battle of Bethel Church...*Anonymous*...........		26
True to his Name ....*Anonymous*..........		27
The South in Arms..........*Rev. J. H. Martin*....		28
God save the South...........*R. S. A.*.............		30
The Tories of Virginia........*Anonymous*..........		31
War-Song...................*A. B. Meek*..........		34
Fort Sumter..................*Anonymous*..........		36
Rebels......................*Anonymous*..........		38
The Heart of Louisiana.......*Harriet Stanton*.......		40
Southern Song of Freedom....*J. H. H.*.............		42

		PAGE
There is nothing going Wrong..*A. M. W.*		44
Maryland, My Maryland......*Jas. R. Randall.*		46
A Cry to Arms...*Anonymous.*		49
War-Song...*Anonymous*		51
The Despot's Song..."*Ole Secesh*"		53
The Southron's War-Song.....*J. A. Wagener.*		55
Justice is our Panoply ..."*De G.*"		56
The Blue Cockade...*Mary W. Crean.*		58
Sweethearts and the War...*Anonymous.*		60
We Come! We Come!...*Millie Mayfield.*		62
Song of the Southern Soldier..*P. E. C.*		64
Lincoln's Inaugural Address..."*A Southern Rights Man*"		66
The Call of Freedom...*Anonymous.*		66
Manassas..."*A Rebel*"		70
Chivalrous C. S. A...*B.*		74
Battle Ode to Virginia...*Anonymous.*		76
The Battle-field of Manassas...*M. F. Bigney.*		77
Flight of Doodles ...*Anonymous.*		86
Confederate Song...*Anonymous.*		89
Destruction of the Vandal Host at Manassas..*J. J. H.*		91
Southern Song...*Anonymous.*		93
Song for the Irish Brigade....."*Shamrock*"		96
Yankee Vandals...*Anonymous.*		98
The South is Up..*P. E. C.*		101
The Old Rifleman...*Frank Ticknor.*		104
The Southern Cross ...*Anonymous.*		106
Up! Up! Set the Stars of our Banner...*M. F. Bigney*		108
Hurrah!..."*A Mississippian*"		109

PAGE

The Soldier-Boy.............*H. M. L.*............ 110
A Southern Gathering Song...*L. Virginia French*... 112
Battle-Call ....*Annie C. Ketchum*.... 114
Another Yankee Doodle.......*Anonymous*.......... 117
The Bonnie Blue Flag ....*Anonymous*.......... 120
The Battle at Bull Run.......*Ruth* 122
The Southron Mother's Charge. *Thomas B. Hood*..... 123
A Call to Kentuckians........*" A Southern Rights
                              Woman "*......... 125
The Stars and Bars...........*Anonymous*.......... 127
King Scare...................*H.*................. 129
Our Braves in Virginia.......*Anonymous*.......... 132
From the South to the North...*C. L. S.*............ 134
My Dream....................*L. F.*............... 137
The Song of the Exile........*B.*.................. 138
The March...................*John W. Overall*..... 141
Southern War-Song...........*N. P. W.*........... 142
We 'll be Free in Maryland....*Robert E. Holtz*...... 145
War-Song....................*J. H. Woodcock*...... 147
A new Red, White, and Blue..*Jeff Thompson*....... 149
O Johnny Bull, my Jo John...*Anonymous*.......... 150
Southrons ....*A Lady of Kentucky*.. 151
" Nil Desperandum "..........*Ada Rose*........... 153
Address of the Women to the
    Southern Troops..........*Mrs. J. T. H. Cross*.. 156
A North Carolina Call to Arms *" Luola "*............ 157
A Southern Woman's Song....*Anonymous*.......... 160
A War-Song for Virginia .....*Anonymous*.......... 162
Land of King Cotton..........*Jo. A. Signaigo*...... 164
Song for the South ....*Anonymous*.......... 165
The Federal Vandals.........*" Senex "*............ 168

PAGE

The Guerillas....................*Anonymous*.......... 169
A Welcome to the Invader. ..*Anonymous*.......... 173
Land of the South.............*A. F. Leonard*....... 174
The Stars and Bars...........*A. J. Requier* 177
North Carolina's War Song....*Anonymous*.......... 179
There 's Life in the Old Land
    Yet......................*Jas. R. Randall*...... 181
The Confederate Flag.........*J. R. Barrick*....... 183
" Stonewall Jackson's Way "..*Anonymous*.......... 185
Burn the Cotton...............*" Estelle "* 187
The Printers of Virginia to
    " Old Abe ".............*Harry C. Treakle*.... 189
The Marseilles Hymn.........*E. F. Porter*........ 191
The Times...................*" Kate "* 194
Thinking of the Soldiers......*Anonymous*.......... 197
A Southern Scene............*Anonymous*.......... 199
Pensacola: To my Son........*M. S*............... 203
The War-Storm...............*C. J. H*............. 205
The Volunteers to the " Melish" *W. C. Estres*........ 207
The Girls of the Monumental
    City.....................*Anonymous*.......... 209
Gone to the Battle-Field ......*John Antrobus*........ 211
The Debt....................*Anonymous*.......... 213
Beyond the Potomac..........*Paul H. Hayne*...... 215
The Confederate Flag.........*Anonymous*.......... 219
The South...................*Charlie Wildwood*.... 220
A Song......................*Anonymous*.......... 222
Battle-Song of the Invaded....*Anonymous*.......... 224
The Turtle...................*Anonymous*.......... 226
Southern Battle-Song.........*Anonymous*.......... 227
Jackson ....*Harry Flash*......... 229

PAGE

Song of the Privateer.........*A. H. Cummins*...... 230
No Union Men................*Millie Mayfield*...... 232
Harp of the South............"*Cora*"............. 234
The Spirits of the Fathers.....*Henry Lomas*........ 235
Heart Victories................"*A Soldier's Wife*".. 238
True-heart Southrons.........*Anonymous*.......... 240
The Irish Battalion...........*Anonymous*.......... 241
Monody on the Death of Stone-
    wall Jackson.............."*The Exile*"........ 244
Rebels.......................*Anonymous*.......... 246
Seventy-Six and Sixty-One...*John W. Overall*..... 248
Kentucky...................."*Estelle*"........... 249
Virginia's Message to the South-
    ern States................*Anonymous*.......... 253
A Poem which needs no Dedi-
    cation....................*Jas. Barron Hope*.... 254
Will you Go?................."*Estelle*"........... 258
God save the South..........*Anonymous*.......... 261
The Battle of the Mississippi...*Anonymous*.......... 262
On! Southron, On!..........*Anonymous*.......... 263
Civile Bellum................*Once a Week*........ 264
War-Song....................*Anonymous*.......... 266
Follow! Boys, Follow!........*Millie Mayfield*...... 269
Bombardment of Vicksburgh..*Anonymous*.......... 272
Lines written in Fort Warren..*Anonymous*.......... 274
The Yankee Devil............*Anonymous*.......... 276
Lines to the Southern Banner..*Anonymous*.......... 279
The Boy Soldier..............*A Lady of Savannah*. 282
The Virginians of the Valley..*Frank Ticknor, M.D.* 284
O, Sweet South...............*W. Gilmore Simms*... 285
The Southern Cross..........*Ellen Key Blunt*..... 287

CONTENTS.

		PAGE
Patriotism	*Anonymous*	289
Song for the Maryland Line	*Anonymous*	290
The South for Me	*Anonymous*	292
Confederate Land	*H. H. Strawbridge*	294
The Song of the South	*Anonymous*	295
The Banner-Song	*James B. Marshall*	297
The Invocation	*B. W. W.*	299

LIST OF AUTHORS.

PAGE

ANTROBUS, JOHN.......................... ... 211

BARRICK, J. R.,............................. 183
BIGNEY, M. F.,..........................77, 108
BLUNT, ELLEN KEY,......................... 287

CREAN, MARY W.,.......................... 58
CROSS, MRS. J. T. H.,........ 156
CUMMINS, A. H.,............................. 230

ESTRES, W. C.,................................. 207

FLASH, HARRY,................................ 229
FRENCH, L. VIRGINIA,....................... 112

HAYNE, PAUL H.,............................ 215
HOLTZ, ROBERT E.,.......................... 145
HOOD, THOMAS B.,.......................... 123
HOPE, JAMES BARRON........................ 254

JACOBUS, MRS. J. J.,......................... 16

KETCHUM, ANNIE CHAMBERS,................ 114

PAGE

LEONARD, A. F., ... 174
LOMAS, HENRY, ... 235

MARSHALL, JAMES B., ... 207
MARTIN, REV. J. H., ... 28
MEEK, A. B., ... 34
MAYFIELD, MILLIE 62, 232

OVERALL, JOHN W., ...23, 141, 248

PIKE, ALBERT, ... 20
PORTER, E. F., ... 191

RANDALL, JAMES R., ...46, 181
REQUIER, A. J., ... 177
ROSE, ADA, ... 153

SIGNAIGO, J. A., ... 164
SIMMS, WM. GILMORE, ... 285
STANTON, HARRIET, ... 40
STRAWBRIDGE, H. H., ... 204

THOMPSON, JOHN R., ... 1
TICKNOR, FRANK, M. D., ...104, 284
TREAKLE, HARRY C., ... 189

WAGENER, J. A., ... 55
WILDWOOD, CHARLES, ... 220
WOODCOCK, J. H., ... 147

REBEL RHYMES AND RHAPSODIES.

A POEM FOR THE TIMES.

BY JOHN R. THOMPSON.

WHO talks of Coercion? Who dares to
    deny
  A resolute people their right to be free?
Let him blot out forever one star from the sky,
  Or curb with his fetter one wave of the sea.

Who prates of Coercion?   Can love be restored
  To bosoms where only resentment may dwell;
Can peace upon earth be proclaimed by the sword,
  Or good-will among men be established by shell?

Shame! shame that the statesman and trickster
    forsooth
  Should have for a crisis no other recourse,
Beneath the fair day-spring of Light and of Truth,
  Than the old *brutem fulmen* of Tyranny,—Force.

1

From the holes where Fraud, Falsehood, and Hate
   slink away;
  From the crypt in which Error lies buried in
   chains;
This foul apparition stalks forth to the day,
  And would ravage the land which his presence
   profanes.

Could you conquer us, Men of the North, could you
   bring
  Desolation and death on our homes as a flood;
Can you hope the pure lily, Affection, will spring
  From ashes all reeking and sodden with blood?

Could you brand us as villains and serfs, know ye
   not
  What fierce, sullen hatred lurks under the scar?
How loyal to Hapsburg is Venice, I wot;
  How dearly the Pole loves his Father, the Czar!

But 't were well to remember this land of the sun
  Is a *nutrix leonum*, and suckles a race
Strong-armed, lion-hearted, and banded as one,
  Who brook not oppression and know not disgrace.

And well may the schemers in office beware
  The swift retribution that waits upon crime,

When the lion, RESISTANCE, shall leap from his
    lair,
  With a fury that renders his vengeance sublime.

Once, men of the North, we were brothers, and
    still,
  Though brothers no more, we would gladly be
    friends;
Nor join in a conflict accurst, that must fill
  With ruin the country on which it descends.

But if smitten with blindness, and mad with the rage
  The gods gave to all whom they wished to de-
    stroy,
You would not act a new Iliad to darken the age,
  With horrors beyond what is told as of Troy:

If, deaf as the adder itself to the cries,
  When Wisdom, Humanity, Justice implore,
You would have our proud eagle to feed on the eyes
  Of those who have taught him so grandly to
    soar:

If there be to your malice no limit imposed,
  And you purpose hereafter to rule with the rod
The men upon whom you have already closed
  Our goodly domain and the temples of God:

To the breeze then your banner dishonored unfold,
　　And at once let the tocsin be sounded afar;
We greet you, as greeted the Swiss Charles the
　　　　Bold,
　　With a farewell to peace and a welcome to war!

For the courage that clings to our soil, ever bright,
　　Shall catch inspirations from turf and from tide:
Our sons unappalled shall go forth to the fight,
　　With the smile of the fair, the pure kiss of the
　　　　bride;

And the bugle its echoes shall send through the
　　　　past,
　　In the trenches of Yorktown to waken the slain;
While the sods of King's Mountain shall heave at
　　　　the blast,
　　And give up its heroes to glory again.
　　　　　　　　　　Charleston Mercury.

HURRYING ON.

ANONYMOUS.

HURRYING on, in the midst of excitement,
　　Pushing extravagant projects through,

Few of us know or pause ever to question,
  Ever to ask where we 're hurrying to ;
Hurrying on over blessings unheeded,
  Chasing some joy, like the butterfly, gone ;
What is the good of our wonderful frenzy ?
  What is the use of our hurrying on ?

We have been hurrying on from our cradles ;
  What but its shadows have we for the Past ?
We are still hurrying on as expectant ;
  What shall we get by our hurry at last ?
Graves are so thick that we cannot well miss them,
  Going with only the clothes we shall wear ;
Where shall be, then, all we 're hurrying after ?
  What shall we have with our hurry when there ?

Hurrying on in the wake of the phantoms,
  Conjured alone in the fever of haste ;
Hurrying on with extravagant projects,
  Little we reck of treasures we waste ;
Little we know of the diamond moments,
  All to be gathered and garnered in store,
Making our worthy or worthless possessions,
  Up in the land where we 'll hurry no more.

Treasures that lie all around us in plenty
  We never heed as we 're hurrying on,

And when in heaven our coffers are empty,
 We shall first know how ·they 're lost and are
   gone ;
Then we shall know how our spirits have wasted
 Wealth of Eternity planted in Time ;
The soil for its seed growing barren as ashes,
 While we are hurrying out of its clime.

God works but slowly, — but slowly, my brothers,
 Not hurrying onward in passion and strife, —
Works with love only, and only for others,
 Not for himself, in the green fields of life ;
Let us sit down, and be calm and be thoughtful,
 Lifting our hearts to eternity's brink ;
Let us cease living alone for the present,
 Let us cease hurrying, — what do you think ?
       Charleston Mercury.
New Orleans, *October* 23, 1861.

A SOUTHERN SONG.

BY " L. M."

IF ever I consent to be married,
 (And who would refuse a good mate ?)
The man whom I give my hand to,
 Must believe in the rights of the State.

To a husband who quietly submits
    To negro -equality sway,
The true Southern girl will not barter
    Her heart and affections away.

The heart I may choose to preside o'er,
    True, warm, and devoted must be,
And have true love for a Union
    Under the Southern Liberty Tree.

Should Lincoln attempt to coerce him
    To share with the negro his right,
Then, smiling, I 'd gird on his armor,
    And bid him God-speed in the fight.

And if he should fall in the conflict,
    His memory with tears I will grace ;
Better weep o'er a patriot fallen,
    Than blush in a Tory embrace.

We girls are all for a Union,
    Where a marked distinction is laid
Between the rights of the mistress
    And those of the kinky-haired maid.

Louisville Courier.

SOUTHERN WAR-CRY.

AIR — " *Scots, wha hae.*"

COUNTRYMEN of Washington !
  Countrymen of Jefferson !
By Old Hick'ry óft led on
    To death or victory !

Sons of men who fought and bled,
Whose blood for you was freely shed,
Where Marion charged and Sumter led,
    For freemen's rights !

From the Cowpens glorious way,
Southron valor led the fray
To Yorktown's eventful day,
    First we were free !

At New Orleans we met the foe ;
Oppressors fell at every blow ;
There we laid the usurper low,
    For maids and wives !

Who on Palo Alto's day,
'Mid fire and hail at Monterey,
At Buena Vista led the way ?
    " Rough-and-Ready ! "

Southrons all, at Freedom's call,
For our homes united all,
Freemen live, or freemen fall!
Death or liberty!

New Orleans Picayune.

———◆———

THE STAR OF THE WEST.

I WISH I was in de land o' cotton,
Old times dair ain't not forgotten, —
    Look away, &c.
In Dixie land whar I was born in,
Early on one frosty mornin', —
    Look away, &c.
      Chorus — Den I wish I was in Dixie.

In Dixie land dat frosty mornin',
Jis 'bout de time de day was dawnin', —
    Look away, &c.
De signal fire from de east bin roarin',
Rouse up, Dixie, no more snorin', —
    Look away, &c.
      Den I wish I was in Dixie.

Dat rocket high a blazing in de sky,
'T is de sign dat de snobbies am comin' up nigh, —
    Look away, &c.

Dey bin braggin' long, if we dare to shoot a shot,
Dey comin' up strong and dey 'll send us all to pot.
    Fire away, fire away, lads in gray.
        Den I wish I was in Dixie.
          Charleston Mercury.

FAREWELL TO BROTHER JONATHAN.

BY CAROLINE.

FAREWELL! we must part; we have turned
    from the land
Of our cold-hearted brother, with tyrannous hand,
Who assumed all our rights as a favor to grant,
And whose smile ever covered the sting of a taunt;

Who breathed on the fame he was bound to de-
    fend, —
Still the craftiest foe, 'neath the guise of a friend;
Who believed that our bosoms would bleed at a
    touch,
Yet could never believe he could goad them too
    much ;

Whose conscience affects to be seared with our sin,
Yet is plastic to take all its benefits in ;

The mote in our eye so enormous has grown,
That he never perceives there 's a beam in his own.

O Jonathan, Jonathan ! vassal of pelf,
Self-righteous, self-glorious, yes, every inch self,
Your loyalty now is all bluster and boast,
But was dumb when the foemen invaded our coast.

In vain did your country appeal to you then,
You coldly refused her your money and men ;
Your trade interrupted, you slunk from her wars,
And preferred British gold to the Stripes and the
      Stars !

Then our generous blood was as water poured
      forth,
And the sons of the South were the shields of the
      North ;
Nor our patriot ardor one moment gave o'er,
Till the foe you had fed we had driven from the
      shore !

Long years we have suffered opprobrium and wrong,
But we clung to your side with affection so strong,
That at last, in mere wanton aggression, you broke
All the ties of our hearts with one murderous
      stroke.

We are tired of contest for what is our own,
We are sick of a strife that could never be done;
Thus our love has died out, and its altars are dark,
Not Prometheus's self could rekindle the spark.

O Jonathan, Jonathan ! deadly the sin
Of your tigerish thirst for the blood of your kin;
And shameful the spirit that gloats over wives
And maidens despoiled of their honor and lives !

Your palaces rise from the fruits of our toil,
Your millions are fed from the wealth of our soil;
The balm of our air brings the health to your cheek,
And our hearts are aglow with the welcome we
    speak.

O brother ! beware how you seek us again,
Lest you brand on your forehead the signet of Cain;
That blood and that crime on your conscience must
    sit;
We may fall — we may perish — but never submit !

The pathway that leads to the Pharisee's door
We remember, indeed, but we tread it no more;
Preferring to turn, with the Publican's faith,
To the path through the valley and shadow of
    death !

"CALL ALL! CALL ALL!"

BY " GEORGIA."

WHOOP! the Doodles have broken loose,
　　Roaring round like the very deuce !
Lice of Egypt, a hungry pack, —
After 'em, boys, and drive 'em back.

Bull-dog, terrier, cur, and fice,
Back to the beggarly land of ice ;
Worry 'em, bite 'em, scratch and tear
Everybody and everywhere.

Old Kentucky is caved from under,
Tennessee is split asunder,
Alabama awaits attack,
And Georgia bristles up her back.

Old John Brown is dead and gone !
Still his spirit is marching on, —
Lantern-jawed, and legs, my boys,
Long as an ape's from Illinois !

Want a weapon ?　Gather a brick,
Club or cudgel, or stone or stick ;
Anything with a blade or butt,
Anything that can cleave or cut.

Anything heavy, or hard, or keen !
Any sort of slaying machine !
Anything with a willing mind,
And the steady arm of a man behind.

Want a weapon ?   Why, capture one !
Every Doodle has got a gun,
Belt, and bayonet, bright and new;
Kill a Doodle, and capture *two !*

Shoulder to shoulder, son and sire !
All, call all ! to the feast of fire !
Mother and maiden, and child and slave,
A common triumph or a single grave.

Rockingham, Va., Register.

—◆—

WHAT THE SOUTH WINDS SAY.

FAINT as the echo of an echo born,
  A bugle-note swells on the air ;
Now louder, fuller, far and near,
  It sounds a mighty horn.

The noblest blast blown in our time
Comes from the South on every breeze,
To sweep across the shining seas
  In symphony sublime !

'T is Freedom's *reveille* that comes
Upon the air, blent with a tramp,
Which tells that she now seats her camp,
    With trumpets and with drums.

When first I heard that pealing horn,
Its sounds were faint and black in the night;
But soon I saw a burst of light
    That told of coming morn!

When first I heard that martial tread
Swell on the chilly morning breeze,
'T was faint as sound of distant seas, —
    Now, it might rouse the dead!

Aye, it has roused the dead! They start
From many a battle-field to teach
Their children noble thoughts and speech, —
    To " fire the Southern heart!"

Not only noble thoughts, but deeds,
Our fathers taught us how to dare;
They fling our banners on the air,
    And bring our battle-steeds!

While louder rings that mighty horn,
Whose clarion notes on every gale

Tells history's latest, greatest tale, —
    A nation now is born !

And at that trump's inspiring peal,
Within Time's lists I see it stand,
A splendid banner in its hand,
    Full armed from head to heel !

Long ages in their flight shall see
That flag wave o'er a nation brave, —
A people who preferred one grave
    Sooner than slavery !

                    Richmond Dispatch.

THE ORDERED AWAY.

Dedicated to the Oglethorpe and Walker Light Infantries.

BY MRS. J. J. JACOBUS.

AT the end of each street, a banner we meet,
    The people all march in a mass,
But quickly aside, they step back with pride,
    To let the brave companies pass.
The streets are dense filled, but the laughter is
            still'd —
The crowd is all going one way;

Their cheeks are blanched white, but they smile as
     they light
   Lift their hats to the — Ordered away.

They smile while the dart deeply pierces their heart,
   But each eye flashes back the war-glance,
As they watch the brave file march up with a smile,
   'Neath their flag, — with their muskets and lance;
The cannon's loud roar vibrates on the shore,
   But the people are quiet to-day,
As, startled, they see how fearless and free
   March the companies — Ordered away.

Not a quiver or gleam of fear can be seen,
   Though they go to meet death in disguise;
For the hot air is filled with poison distilled
   'Neath the rays of fair Florida's skies.
Hark! the drum and fife awake to new life
   The soldiers who — " Can't get away; "
Who *wish*, as they wave their hats to the brave,
   That *they* were the — Ordered away.

As *our* parting grows near, let us quell back the
     tear, —
   Let our smiles shine as bright as of yore;
Let us stand with the mass, salute as they pass,
   And weep when we see them no more.

2

Let no tear-drop or sigh dim the light of our eye,
  Or move from our lips — as they say — ·
While waving our hand to a brave little band,
  Good-by, to the — Ordered away.

Let them go, in God's name, in defence of their *fame*,
  Brave death at the cannon's wide mouth ;
Let them honor and save the land of the brave,
  Plant Freedom's bright flag in the *South*.
Let them go ! While we weep, and lone vigils
      keep,
  We will bless them, and fervently pray
To the God whom we trust, for our cause firm but
      just,
  And our loved ones — the Ordered away.

When fierce battles storm, we will rise up each
      morn,
  Teach our young sons the sabre to wield :
Should their brave fathers die, we will arm *them* to
      fly
  And fill up the gap in the field.
Then, fathers and brothers, fond husbands and
      lovers,
  March ! march bravely on ! *We* will stay,
Alone in our sorrow, to pray on each morrow
  For our loved ones — the Ordered away.

AUGUSTA, GA., *April* 2, 1861.

THE MARTYR OF ALEXANDRIA.

REVEAL'D, as in a lightning flash,
    A Hero stood!
Th' invading foe, the trumpet's crash,
    Set up his blood!

High o'er the sacred pile that bends
    Those forms above,
Thy Star, O Freedom! brightly blends
    Its rays with Love.

The banner of a mighty race
    Serenely there
Unfurls, — the genius of the place,
    And haunted air!

A vow is registered in heaven —
    Patriot! 't was thine
To guard those matchless colors, given
    By hand Divine.

Jackson! thy spirit may not hear
    The wail ascend!
A nation bends above thy bier,
    And mourns its friend.

Th' example is thy monument;
      In organ tones
Thy name resounds, with glory blent,
      Prouder than thrones !

And they whose loss has been our gain —
      A People's care
Shall win their hearts from pain,
      And wipe the tear.

When time shall set the captives free,
      Now scath'd by wrath, —
Heirs of his immortality,
      Bright be their path.

Indianola, Texas.   J. W. S.

———◆———

DIXIE.

SOUTHRONS, HEAR YOUR COUNTRY CALL YOU !

BY ALBERT PIKE.

SOUTHRONS, hear your Country call you !
   Up ! lest worse than death befall you !
      To arms ! To arms ! To arms ! in Dixie !
Lo ! all the beacon-fires are lighted,
Let all hearts be now united !

To arms! To arms! To arms! in Dixie!
Advance the flag of Dixie!
Hurrah! hurrah!
For Dixie's land we take our stand,
And live or die for Dixie!
To arms! To arms!
And conquer peace for Dixie!
To arms! To arms!
And conquer peace for Dixie!

Hear the Northern thunders mutter!
Northern flags in South wind flutter;
To arms, etc.
Advance the flag of Dixie! etc.

Fear no danger! Shun no labor!
Lift up rifle, pike, and sabre!
To arms, etc.
Shoulder pressing close to shoulder,
Let the odds make each heart bolder!
To arms, etc.
Advance the flag of Dixie! etc.

How the South's great heart rejoices,
At your cannons' ringing voices ;
To arms! etc.
For faith betrayed and pledges broken,

Wrongs inflicted, insults spoken;
　　To arms! etc.
　　　　Advance the flag of Dixie! etc.

Strong as lions, swift as eagles,
Back to their kennels hunt these beagles;
　　To arms! etc.
Cut the unequal words asunder!
Let them then each other plunder!
　　To arms! etc.
　　　　Advance the flag of Dixie! etc.

Swear upon your Country's altar,
Never to submit or falter;
　　To arms! etc.
Till the spoilers are defeated,
Till the Lord's work is completed.
　　To arms! etc.
　　　　Advance the flag of Dixie! etc.

Halt not, till our Federation
Secures among Earth's Powers its station!
　　To arms! etc.
Then at peace, and crowned with glory,
Hear your children tell the story!
　　To arms! etc.
　　　　Advance the flag of Dixie! etc.

If the loved ones weep in sadness,
Victory soon shall bring them gladness :
　　To arms ! etc.
Exultant pride soon banish sorrow ;
Smiles chase tears away to-morrow.
　　To arms ! etc.
　　　Advance the flag of Dixie ! etc.

——◆——

THE RIGHT ABOVE THE WRONG.

BY JOHN W. OVERALL.

IN other days our fathers' love was loyal, full, and
　　free,
For those they left behind them in the Island of the
　　Sea ;
They fought the battles of King George, and toasted
　　him in song,
For then the Right kept proudly down the tyranny
　　of Wrong.

But when the King's weak, willing slaves laid tax
　　upon the tea,
The Western men rose up and braved the Island
　　of the Sea ;
And swore a fearful oath to God, those men of iron
　　might,

That in the end the Wrong should die, and up
    should go the Right.

The King sent over hireling hosts, — Briton, Hes-
    sian, Scot, —
And swore in turn those Western men, when cap-
    tured, should be shot ;
While Chatham spoke with earnest tongue against
    the hireling throng,
And mournfully saw the Right go down, and place
    give to the Wrong.

But God was on the righteous side, and Gideon's
    sword was out,
With clash of steel, and rattling drum, and free-
    man's thunder-shout ;
And crimson torrents drenched the land through
    that long, stormy fight,
But in the end, hurrah ! the Wrong was beaten by
    the Right !

And when again the foemen came from out the
    Northern Sea,
To desolate our smiling land and subjugate the free,
Our fathers rushed to drive them back, with rifles
    keen and long,
And swore a mighty oath, the Right should subju-
    gate the Wrong.

And while the world was looking on, the strife
    uncertain grew,
But soon aloft rose up our stars amid a field of
    blue ;
For Jackson fought on red Chalmette, and won the
    glorious fight,
And then the Wrong went down, hurrah ! and
    triumph crowned the Right !

The day has come again, when men who love the
    beauteous South,
To speak, if needs be, for the Right, though by the
    cannon's mouth ;
For foes accursed of God and man, with lying
    speech and song,
Would bind, imprison, hang the Right, and deify
    the Wrong.

But canting knave of pen and sword, nor sancti-
    monious fool,
Shall never win this Southern land, to cripple, bind,
    and rule ;
We 'll muster on each bloody plain, thick as the
    stars of night,
And, through the help of God, the Wrong shall
    perish by the Right.

New Orleans True Delta.

THE BATTLE OF BETHEL CHURCH.

JUNE 10, 1861.

A S hurtles the tempest,
  Proclaiming the storm,
The Northern invaders
  Tumultuously swarm.
Loudly rings their battle-cry,
Glares with fury every eye;
Virginia's sons they swear shall die,
  Or wear their chains of slavery.

As meets the chafed ocean
  The immutable rock,
The brave Southern freemen
  Await the stern shock.
Firm is every lip compressed,
Front to foe is every breast,
While silent prayer to Heaven attest
  Resolve for death or victory.

They number by thousands,
  The men that assail;
The hundreds that wait them,
  Oh! can they prevail?
Spoils and beauty urge the fray,
Hearts and homes contest the day,

And fiercely brands the battle's bray,
  While Right and Might strive valiantly.

Down sweep the invaders,
   Like billows of storm,—
Dead, wounded, and dying,
   They backward are borne.
Vain they rally, vain return,—
Lead and steel and graves they earn; ·
While angels guard their ranks from harm
  Who fight for homes and liberty.

See! see! they are flying!
   Quick, up and pursue!
And mete out the measure
   The hirelings due!
Wolves, as brave, to sheepfolds hie;
Lambs, less swift, from lions fly;
While thanks ascend to Him on high
  Who gave our arms the victory.

                  New Orleans Delta.

TRUE TO HIS NAME.

IN ancient days, Jehovah said,
  In voice both sweet and calm,

Be Abram's name forever changed
  To that of Abraham!

'T was then decreed his progeny
  Should occupy high stations,
For Abraham, in Hebrew, means
  " Father of many nations !"

In our own land an Abraham,
  With speeches wise nor witty,
Went down to our Jerusalem,
  The famous Federal city.

True to his name, this Abraham,
  So changed are his relations,
Instead of one great nation, be
  " Father of many nations."

New Orleans True Delta.

THE SOUTH IN ARMS.

BY REV. J. H. MARTIN.

OH ! see ye not the sight sublime,
  Unequalled in all previous time,
Presented in this Southern clime,
        The home of chivalry ?

A warlike race of freemen stand,
With martial front and sword in hand,
Defenders of their native land, —
    The sons of Liberty.

Unawed by numbers, they defy
The tyrant North, nor will they fly,
Resolved to conquer or to die,
    And win a glorious name.

Sprung from renowned heroic sires,
Inflamed with patriotic fires,
Their bosoms burn with fierce desires,
    The thirst for victory.

'T is not the love of bloody strife,
The horrid sacrifice of life,
But thoughts of mother, sister, wife,
    That stir their manly hearts.

A sense of honor bids them go,
To meet a hireling, ruthless foe,
And deal in wrath the deadly blow
    Which vengeance loud demands.

In Freedom's sacred cause they fight,
For Independence, Justice, Right,

And to resist a desperate might.
And by Manassas' glorious name,
And by Missouri's fields of fame,
We hear them swear, with one acclaim,
    We 'll triumph, or we 'll die !

———◆———

GOD SAVE THE SOUTH !

BY R. S. A.

WAKE, every minstrel strain !
    Ring o'er each Southern plain —
God save the South !
Still let this noble band,
Joined now in heart and hand,
Fight for our sunny land, —
    Land of the South.

Armed in such sacred cause,
We covet no vain applause ;
    Our swords are free.
No spot of wrong or shame
Rests on our banner's fame,
Flung forth in Freedom's name
    O'er mound and sea.

Then let the invader come ;
Soon will the beat of drum
    Rally us all.
Forth from our homes we go —
Death ! death ! to every foe ;
Says each maiden low :
    God save us all !

Ay, when the battle-hour
Darkest may seem to lower,
    God is our trust.

———◆———

TO THE TORIES OF VIRGINIA.

"I speak this unto your shame."

IN the ages gone by, when Virginia arose
    Her honor and truth to maintain,
Her sons round her banner would rally with pride,
    Determined to save it from stain.

No heart in those days was so false or so cold,
    That it did not exquisitely thrill
With a love and devotion that none would withhold,
    Until death the proud bosom should chill.

Was Virginia in danger ?   Fast, fast at her call,
  From the mountains e'en unto the sea,
Came up her brave children their mother to shield,
  And to die that she still might be free.

And a coward was he, who, when danger's dark
       cloud
  Overshadowed Virginia's fair sky,
Turned a deaf, careless ear, when her summons was
       heard,
  Or refused for her honor to die.

Oh ! proud are the mem'ries of days that are past,
  And richly the heart thrills whene'er
We think of the brave, who, their mother to save,
  Have died, as they lived, without fear.

But, *now*, can it be that Virginia's name
  Fails to waken the homage and love
Of e'en one of her sons ?   Oh ! cold, cold must be
  The heart that her name will not move.

When she rallies for freedom, for justice, and
      right,
  Will her sons, with a withering sneer,
Revile her, and taunt her with treason and shame,
  Or say she is moved by foul fear ?

Will they tell her her glories have fled or grown pale ?
    That she bends to a tyrant in shame ?
Will they trample her glorious flag in the dust,
    Or load with reproaches her name ?

Will they fly from her shores, or desert her in need ?
    Will *Virginians* their backs ever turn
On their mother, and fly when the danger is nigh,
    And her claim to their fealty spurn ?

False, false is the heart that refuses to yield
    The love that Virginia doth claim ;
And base is the tongue that could utter the lie,
    That charges his mother with shame.

A blot on her 'scutcheon ! a stain on her name !
    Our heart's blood should wipe it away ;
We should die for her honor, and count it a boon
    Her mandates to heed and obey.

But never, oh, never, let human tongue say
    She is false to her honor or fame !
She is true to her past — to her future she 's true —
    And Virginia has never known shame.

Then shame on the dastard, the recreant fool,
    That *would strike, in the dark,* at her now ;

That would coldly refuse her fair fame to uphold,
 That would basely prove false to his vow..

But no ! it cannot — it can never be true,
 That Virginia claims one single child,
That would ever prove false to his home or his God,
 Or be with foul treason defiled.

And the man that could succor her enemies *now,*
 Even though on her soil he were born,
Is so base, so inhuman, so false, and so vile,
 That Virginia disowns him with scorn !

Richmond Examiner.

WAR SONG.

BY A. B. MEEK, OF MOBILE.

WOULDST thou have me love thee, dearest,
 With a woman's proudest heart,
Which shall ever hold thee nearest,
 Shrined in its inmost part ?

Listen, then ! My country's calling
 On her sons to meet the foe !
Leave these groves of rose and myrtle,
 Drop the dreamy hand of love !

Like young Körner, scorn the turtle
  When the eagle screams above !
Dost thou pause ?   Let dotards dally —
  Do thou for thy country fight !

'Neath her noble emblem rally —
  " God ! our country, and her right ! "
Listen ! now her trumpet 's calling
  On her sons to meet the foe !

Woman's heart is soft and tender,
  But 't is proud and faithful, too ;
Shall she be her land's defender ?
  Lover ! soldier ! up and do !

Seize thy father's ancient falchion,
  Which once flashed as freedom's star !
Till sweet peace — the bow and halcyon,
  Still'd the stormy strife of war !

Listen ! now thy country 's calling
  On her sons to meet the foe !
Sweet is love in moonlight bowers !
  Sweet the altar and the flame !

Sweet is spring-time with her flowers !
  Sweeter far the patriot's name !

Should the God who rules above thee
Doom thee to a soldier's grave,

Hearts will break, but fame will love thee,
Canonized among the brave !
Listen, then, thy country 's calling
On her sons to meet her foe !

Rather would I view thee lying
On the last red field of life,
'Mid thy country's heroes dying,
Than to be a dastard's wife.

———◆———

FORT SUMTER.

IT was a noble Roman,
  In Rome's imperial day,
Who heard a coward croaker
  Before the battle say :
" They 're safe in such a fortress ;
  There is no way to shake it ; " —
" On ! on ! " exclaimed the hero,
  " I 'LL FIND A WAY, OR MAKE IT ! "

Is FAME your aspiration ?
  Her path is steep and high ;

In vain he seeks the temple,
　Content to gaze and sigh ;
The crowded town is waiting,
　But he *alone* can take it,
Who says, with " SOUTHERN FIRMNESS,"
　" I 'LL FIND A WAY, OR MAKE IT !"

Is GLORY your ambition ?
　There is no royal road ;
Alike we all must labor,
　Must climb to her abode ;
Who feels the thirst for *glory*,
　In Helicon may slake it,
If he has but the " SOUTHERN WILL,"
　" TO FIND A WAY, OR MAKE IT !"

Is SUMTER worth the getting ?
　It must be bravely sought ;
With wishing and with fretting
　The boon cannot be bought ;
To *all* the prize is open,
　But only he can take it,
Who says, with " SOUTHERN COURAGE,"
　" I 'LL FIND A WAY, OR MAKE IT !"

In all impassioned warfare,
　The tale has ever been,

That victory crowns the valiant;
  The brave are they who win.
Though strong in " *Sumter Fortress,*"
  A HERO still may take it,
Who says, with " SOUTHERN DARING,"
  " I 'LL FIND A WAY, OR MAKE IT ! "

Charleston Mercury.

———◆———

REBELS.

REBELS ! 't is a holy name !
  The name our fathers bore,
When battling in the cause of Right,
Against the tyrant in his might,
  In the dark days of yore.

Rebels ! 't is our family name !
  Our father, Washington,
Was the arch-rebel in the fight,
And gave the name to us, — a right
  Of father unto son.

Rebels ! 't is our given name !
  Our mother, Liberty,
Received the title with her fame,

In days of grief, of fear, and shame,
  When at her breast were we.

Rebels ! 't is our sealed name !
  A baptism of blood !
The war — aye, and the din of strife —
The fearful contest, life for life —
  The mingled crimson flood.

Rebels ! 't is a patriot's name !
  In struggles it was given ;
We bore it then when tyrants raved
And through their curses 't was engraved
  On the doomsday-book of heaven.

Rebels ! 't is our fighting name !
  For peace rules o'er the land,
Until they speak of craven woe —
Until our rights receive a blow,
  From foe's or brother's hand.

Rebels ! 't is our dying name !
  For, although life is dear,
Yet, freemen born and freemen bred,
We 'd rather live as freemen dead,
  Than live in slavish fear.

Then call us rebels, if you will —
  We glory in the name ;
For bending under unjust laws,
And swearing faith to an unjust cause,
  We count a greater shame.

Atlanta Confederacy.

----♦----

THE HEART OF LOUISIANA.

BY HARRIET STANTON.

OH ! let me weep, while o'er our land
  Vile discord strides, with sullen brow,
And drags to earth, with ruthless hand,
  The flag no tyrant's power could bow !

Trailed in the dust, inglorious laid,
  While one by one her stars retire,
And pride and power pursue the raid,
  That bids our liberty expire.

Aye, let me weep ! for surely Heaven
  In anger views the unholy strife ;
And angels weep that thus is riven
  The tie that gave to Freedom life.

I cannot shout — I will not sing
   Loud pæans o'er a severed tie ;
And draped in woe, in tears I fling
   Our State's new flag to greet the sky.

I can but choose, while senseless zeal
   And lawless hate is clothed with power,
The bitter cup ; but still I feel
   The sadness of this parting hour !

I know that thousand hearts will bleed
   While loud huzzas the welkin rend;
The thoughtless crowd will shout, Secede !
   But ah ! will this the conflict end ?

Oh ! let me weep and prostrate lie
   Low at the footstool of my God;
I cannot breathe one note of joy,
   While yet I feel His chastening rod.

Sure, we have as a nation sinned —
   Let every heart its folly own,
And sackcloth, as a girdle bind,
   And mourn our glorious Union gone !

Sisters, farewell ! You know not half
   The pain your pride, injustice, give ;

You spurn our cause, and lightly laugh,
  And hope no more the wrong shall live.
New Orleans Delta.

SOUTHERN SONG OF FREEDOM.

Air — "*The Minstrel's Return.*"

A NATION has sprung into life
  Beneath the bright Cross of the South ;
And now a loud call to the strife
  Rings out from the shrill bugle's mouth.
They gather from morass and mountain,
  They gather from prairie and mart,
To drink, at young Liberty's fountain,
  The nectar that kindles the heart.
    Then, hail to the land of the pine !
      The home of the noble and free ;
    A palmetto wreath we 'll entwine
      Round the altar of young Liberty !

Our flag, with its cluster of stars,
  Firm fixed in a field of pure blue,
All shining through red and white bars,
  Now gallantly flutters in view.
The stalwart and brave round it rally,
  They press to their lips every fold,

While the hymn swells from hill and from valley,
  "Be God with our Volunteers bold."
        Then, hail to the land of the pine! &c.

Th' invaders rush down from the North,
  Our borders are black with their hordes;
Like wolves for their victims they flock,
  While whetting their knives and their swords.
Their watchword is " Booty and Beauty,"
  Their aim is to steal as they go;
But, Southrons, act up to your duty,
  And lay the foul miscreants low.
        Then, hail to the land of the pine! &c.

The God of our fathers looks down
  And blesses the cause of the just;
His smile will the patriot crown
  Who tramples his chains in the dust.
March, march Southrons! shoulder to shoulder,
  One heart-throb, one shout for the cause;
Remember — the world's a beholder,
  And your bayonets are fixed at your doors!
        Then, hail to the land of the pine!
          The home of the noble and free;
          A palmetto wreath we 'll entwine
            Round the altar of young Liberty.

J. H. H.

THERE 'S NOTHING GOING WRONG.

Dedicated to " Old Abe."

THERE 'S a general alarm,
　The South 's begun to arm,
And every hill and glen
Pours forth its warrior men ;
Yet, " There 's nothing going wrong,"
Is the burden of my song.

Six States already out,
Beckon others on the route ;
And the cry is " Still they come ! "
From the Southern sunny home ;
Yet, " There 's nothing going wrong,"
Is the burden of my song.

There 's a wail in the land,
From a want-stricken band ;
And " Food ! Food ! " is the cry :
" Give us work or we die ! "
Yet, " There 's nothing going wrong,"
Is the burden of my song.

The sturdy farmer doth complain
Of low prices for his grain ;

And the miller, with his flour,
Murmurs the dulness of the hour.
Yet, " There 's nothing going wrong,"
Is the burden of my song.

The burly butcher in the mart,
He, too, also takes his part ;
And the merchant in his store
Hears no creaking of his door ;
But " There 's nothing going wrong,"
Is the burden of my song.

Stagnation is everywhere ;
On the water, in the air,
In the shop, in the forge,
On the mount, in the gorge ;
With the anvil, with the loom,
In the store and counting-room ;
In the city, in the town,
With Mr. Smith, with Mr. Brown !
And " yet there 's nothing wrong,"
Is the burden of my song.   A. M. W.

NEW ORLEANS, *March* 4, 1861.

MARYLAND.

BY JAMES R. RANDALL.

THE despot's heel is on thy shore,
    Maryland !
His torch is at thy temple door,
    Maryland !
Avenge the patriotic gore
That flecked the streets of Baltimore,
And be the battle-queen of yore,
    Maryland ! My Maryland !

Hark to wand'ring son's appeal,
    Maryland !
My mother State ! to thee I kneel,
    Maryland !
For life and death, for woe and weal,
Thy peerless chivalry reveal,
And gird thy beauteous limbs with steel,
    Maryland ! My Maryland !

Thou wilt not cower in the dust,
    Maryland !
Thy beaming sword shall never rust,
    Maryland !
Remember Carroll's sacred trust ;

Remember Howard's warlike thrust, —
And all thy slumberers with the just,
   Maryland!   My Maryland!

Come! 't is the red dawn of the day,
   Maryland!
Come! with thy panoplied array,
   Maryland!
With Ringgold's spirit for the fray,
With Watson's blood, at Monterey,
With fearless Lowe, and dashing May,
   Maryland!   My Maryland!

Come! for thy shield is bright and strong,
   Maryland!
Come! for thy dalliance does thee wrong,
   Maryland!
Come! to thine own heroic throng,
That stalks with Liberty along,
And give a new *Key* to thy song,
   Maryland!   My Maryland!

Dear Mother! burst the tyrant's chain,
   Maryland!
Virginia should not call in vain,
   Maryland!
She meets her sisters on the plain:

" *Sic semper*," 't is the proud refrain,
That baffles minions back amain,
　　　Maryland !
Arise, in majesty again,
　　　Maryland !　My Maryland !

I see the blush upon thy cheek,
　　　Maryland !
But thou wast ever bravely meek,
　　　Maryland !
But lo ! there surges forth a shriek
From hill to hill, from creek to creek, —
Potomac calls to Chesapeake,
　　　Maryland !　My Maryland !

Thou wilt not yield the Vandal toll,
　　　Maryland !
Thou wilt not crook to his control,
　　　Maryland !
Better the fire upon thee roll,
Better the blade, the shot, the bowl,
Than crucifixion of the soul,
　　　Maryland !　My Maryland !

I hear the distant thunder hum,
　　　Maryland !
The Old Line's bugle, fife and drum,
　　　Maryland !

She is not dead, nor deaf, nor dumb:
Huzza! she spurns the Northern scum!
She breathes — she burns! she 'll come! she 'll
      come!
Maryland! My Maryland!
POINTE COUPEE, *April* 26, 1861.

----✦----

A CRY TO ARMS.

HO! woodsmen of the mountain side!
   Ho! dwellers in the vales!
Ho! ye who by the chafing tide
   Have roughened in the gales!
Leave barn and byre, leave kin and cot,
   Lay by the bloodless spade;
Let desk, and case, and counter rot,
   And burn your books of trade!

The despot roves your fairest lands;
   And, till he flies or fears,
Your fields must grow but armed hands,
   Your sheaves be sheaves of spears!
Give up to mildew and to rust
   The useless tools of gain,
And feed your country's sacred dust
   With floods of crimson rain!

Come, with the weapons at your call, —
  With musket, pike, or knife;
He wields the deadliest blade of all
  Who lightest holds his life.
The arm that drives its unbought blows,
  With all a patriot's scorn,
Might brain a tyrant with a rose,
  Or stab him with a thorn!

Does any falter? Let him turn
  To some brave maiden's eyes,
And catch the holy fires that burn
  In those sublunar skies.
Oh! could you like your women feel,
  And in their spirit march,
A day might see your lines of steel
  Beneath the victor's arch.

What hope, O God! would not grow warm,
  When thoughts like these give cheer?
The Lily calmly braves the storm,
  And shall the Palm-tree fear?
No! rather let its branches court
  The rack that sweeps the plain,
And from the Lily's regal port
  Learn how to breast the strain!

Ho! woodsmen of the mountain side!
  Ho! dwellers in the vales!
Ho! ye who by the roaring tide
  Have roughened in the gales!
Come! flocking gayly to the fight,
  From forest, hill, and lake;
We battle for our Country's right,
  And for the Lily's sake!
      New Orleans, *March* 9, 1862.

------◆------

WAR SONG.*

Air — "*March, march, Ettrick and Teviotdale.*"

MARCH, march on, brave "Palmetto" boys,
  "Sumter" and "Lafayettes," forward
      in order;
March, march, "Calhoun" and "Rifle" boys,
  All the base Yankees are crossing the *border.*
      Banners are round ye spread,
      Floating above your head,
Soon shall the *Lone Star* be famous in story,
      On, on, my gallant men,

* The writer has a husband, three sons, two nephews,
other relatives and friends, in the companies mentioned,
to whom these lines are most respectfully inscribed. —
Charleston Mercury.

Vict'ry be thine again ;
Fight for your *rights*, till the green sod is gory.
　　　　　　　March, march, &c.

Young wives and sisters have buckled your armor
　　on ;
Maidens ye love bid ye *go* to the battle-field;
Strong arms and stout hearts have many a vict'ry
　　won,
　Courage shall strengthen the weapons ye wield.
　　Wild passions are storming,
　　Dark schemes are forming,
Deep snares are laid, but they *shall not* enthrall
　　ye ;
　　Justice your cause shall greet,
　　Laurels lay at your feet,
If each brave band be but watchful and wary.
　　　　　　　March, march, &c.

Let fear and unmanliness vanish before ye ;
　Trust in the Rock who will shelter the right-
　　eous ;
Plant *firmly* each step on the soil of the *free*, —
　A heritage left by the sires who bled for us.
　　May each heart be bounding,
　　When trumpets are sounding,
And the dark traitors shall strive to surround ye ;

The great God of Battle
Can *still* the war-rattle,
And brighten the land with a sunset of glory.
March, march, &c.

THE DESPOT'S SONG.

BY " OLE SECESH."

WITH a beard that was filthy and red,
His mouth with tobacco bespread,
Abe Lincoln sat in the gay White House,
A-wishing that he was dead, —
Swear! swear! swear!
Till his tongue was blistered o'er;
Then, in a voice not very strong,
He slowly whined the Despot's song : —

Lie! lie! lie!
I 've lied like the very deuce!
Lie! lie! lie!
As long as lies were of use;
But now that lies no longer pay,
I know not where to turn;
For when I the truth would say,
My tongue with lies will burn!

Drink ! drink ! drink !
Till my head feels very queer !
Drink ! drink ! drink !
Till I get rid of all fear !
Brandy, and whiskey, and gin,
   Sherry, and champagne, and pop,
I tipple, I guzzle, I suck 'em all in,
   Till down dead-drunk I drop.

Think ! think ! think !
Till my head is very sore !
Think ! think ! think !
Till I could n't think any more !
And it 's oh ! to be splitting of rails,
   Back in my Illinois hut ;
For now that everything fails,
   I would of my office be " shut ! "

Jeff. ! Jeff. ! Jeff. !
To you as a suppliant I kneel !
Jeff. ! Jeff. ! Jeff. !
If you could *my* horrors feel,
You 'd submit at discretion,
   And kindly give in
To all my oppression,
   My weakness and sin !

THE SOUTHRON'S WAR-SONG.

BY J. A. WAGENER.

ARISE! arise! with main and might,
   Sons of the sunny clime!
Gird on the sword; the sacred fight
   The holy hour doth chime.
Arise! the craven host draws nigh,
   In thundering array;
Arise, ye brave! let cowards fly —
   The hero bides the fray.

Strike hard, strike hard, thou noble band;
   Strike hard, with arm of fire!
Strike hard, for God and fatherland,
   For mother, wife, and sire!
Let thunders roar, the lightning flash;
   Bold Southron, never fear!
The bay'net's point, the sabre's clash,
   True Southrons do and dare!

Bright flow'rs spring from the hero's grave;
   The craven knows no rest!
Thrice curs'd the traitor and the knave!
   The hero thrice is bless'd.

Then let each noble Southron stand,
  With bold and manly eye :
We 'll do for God and fatherland ;
  We 'll do, we 'll do, or die !

Charleston Courier.

JUSTICE IS OUR PANOPLY.

BY DE G.

WE 'RE free from Yankee despots,
  We 've left the foul mud-sills,
Declared for e'er our freedom, —
  We 'll keep it spite of ills.

Bring forth your scum and rowdies,
  Thieves, vagabonds, and all ;
March down your Seventh Regiment,
  Battalions great and small.

We 'll meet you in Virginia,
  A Southern battle-field,
Where Southern men will never
  To Yankee foemen yield.

Equip your Lincoln cavalry,
  Your NEGRO *light*-brigade,

Your hodmen, bootblacks, tinkers,
 And scum of every grade.

Pretended love for negroes
 Incites you to the strife ;
Well, come each Yankee white man,
 And take a negro wife.

You 'd make fit black companions,
 Black heart joined to black skin ;
Such *unions* would be glorious —
 They 'd make the Devil grin.

Our freedom is our panoply —
 Come on, you base *black*-guards,
We 'll snuff you like wax-candles,
 Led by our Beauregards.

P. G. T. B. is not alone,
 Men like him with him fight ;
God's providence is o'er us,
 He will protect the right.

THE BLUE COCKADE.

BY MARY WALSINGHAM CREAN.

GOD be with the laddie, who wears the blue
  cockade!
 He's gone to fight the battles of our darling
   Southern land;
He was true to old Columbia, till more sacred ties
  forbade —
 Till 't were treason to obey her, when he took
   his sword in hand;
And God be with the laddie, who was true in heart
  and hand,
To the voice of old Columbia, till she wronged
  his native land!

He buckled on his knapsack — his musket on his
  breast —
 And donned the plumèd bonnet — sword and
   pistol by his side;
Then his weeping mother kissed him, and his aged
  father bless'd,
 And he pinned the floating ribbon to his gallant
   plume of pride.
And God be with the ribbon, and the floating
  plume of pride!
They have gone where duty called them, and may
  glory them betide!

He would not soil his honor, and he would not
    strike a blow,
  For he loved the aged Union, and he breath'd
    no taunting word ;
He would dare Columbia, till she swore herself his
    foe, —
  Forged the chains for freemen—when he buckled
    on his sword.
And God be with the freeman, when he buckled on
    his sword !
He lives or dies for duty, and he yields no inch
    of sward.

The foes they come with thunder, and with blood
    and fire arrayed,
  And they swear that we shall own them, — they
    the masters, we the slaves;
But there's many a gallant laddie, who wears a
    blue cockade,
  Will show them what it is to dare the blood of
    Southern braves !
And God be with the banner of those gallant
    Southern braves !
They may nobly die as freemen — they can never
    live as slaves !

SWEETHEARTS AND THE WAR.

OH, dear! it's shameful, I declare,
　To make the men all go
And leave so many sweethearts here
　Without a single beau.
We like to see them brave, 't is true,
　And would not urge them stay;
But what are we, poor girls, to do
　When they are all away?

We told them we could spare them there,
　Before they had to go;
But, bless their hearts, we were n't aware
　That we should miss them so.
We miss them all, in many ways,
　But truth will ever out,
The greatest thing we miss them for
　Is seeing us about.

On Sunday, when we go to church,
　We look in vain for some
To meet us, smiling, on the porch,
　And ask to see us home.
And then, we can't enjoy a walk
　Since all the beaux have gone,

For what's the good, (to use plain talk,)
  If we must trudge alone?

But what's the use of talking thus?
  We'll try to be content;
And if they cannot come to us,
  A message may be sent.
And that's one comfort, any way;
  For though we are apart,
There is no reason why we may
  Not open heart to heart.

We trust it may soon come
  To a final test;
We want to see our Southern homes
  Secured in peaceful rest.
But if the blood of those we love
  In Freedom's cause must flow,
With fervent trust in God above,
  We bid them onward go.

And we will watch them, as they go,
  And cheer them on their way;
Our arms shall be their resting-place
  When wounded sore they lay.
Oh! if the sons of Southern soil
  For Freedom's cause must die,

Her daughters ask no dearer boon
Than by their side to lie.

———◆———

" WE COME! WE COME!"

BY MILLIE MAYFIELD.*

WE come! we come, for Death or Life,
   For the Grave or Victory !
We come to the broad Red Sea of strife,
   Where the black flag waveth free !
We come as Men, to do or die,
   Nor feel that the lot is hard,
When *our* Hero calls — and our battle-cry
   Is " On, to Beauregard ! "

Up, craven, up ! 't is no time for ease,
   When the crimson war-tide rolls
To our very doors — up, up, for these
   Are times to try men's souls !
The purple gore calls from the sod
   Of our martyred brothers' graves,
And raises a red right hand to God
   To guard our avenging braves.

* Dedicated to the Crescent Regiment, of New Orleans,
Col. M. J. Smith.

And unto the last bright drop that thrills
   The depths of the Southern heart,
We must battle for our sunny hills,
   For the freedom of our Mart —
For all that Honor claims, or Right —
   For Country, Love, and Home!
Shout to the trampling steeds of Might
   Our cry — " We come! we come!"

And let our path through their serried ranks
   Be the fierce tornado's track,
That bursts from the torrid's fervid banks
   And scatters destruction black!
For the hot life leaping in the veins
   Of our young Confederacy,
Must break for aye the galling chains
   Of dark-brow'd Treachery.

On! on! 't is our gallant chieftain calls,
   (He must not call in vain,)
For aid to guard his homestead walls —
   Our Hero of the Plain!
We come! we come, to do or die,
   Nor feel that the lot is hard : —
" God and our Rights!" be our battle-cry,
   And, " On, to Beauregard!"

SONG OF THE SOUTHERN SOLDIER.

BY P. E. C.

TUNE. — "*Barclay and Perkins' Drayman.*"

I 'M a soldier, you see, that oppression has made !
   I don't fight for pay or for booty ;
But I wear in my hat a blue cockade,
   Placed there by the fingers of Beauty.
The South is my home, where a black man is black,
   And a white man there is a white man ;
Now I 'm tired of listening to Northern clack, —
   Let us see what they 'll do in a fight, man.

The Yankees are cute ; they have managed some-
      how
   Their business and ours to settle ;
They make all we want, from a pin to a plough,
   Now we 'll show them some Southern metal.
We have had just enough of their Northern law,
   That robbed us so long of our right, man,
And too much of their cursed abolition jaw, —
   Now we 'll see what they 'll do in a fight, man !

Their parsons will open their sanctified jaws,
   And cant of our slave-growing sin, sir ;
They pocket the *profits*, while preaching the laws,
   And manage our cotton to spin, sir.

Their incomes are nice, on our sugar and rice,
    Though against it the hypocrites write, sir ;
Now our dander is up, and they 'll soon smell a
      mice,
    If we once get them into a fight, sir.

Our cotton bales once made a good barricade,
    And can still do the State a good service ;
With them and the boys of the blue cockade,
    There is power enough to preserve us.
So shoulder your rifles, my boys, for defence,
    In the cause of our freedom and right, man ;
If there 's no other way for to learn them sense,
    We may teach them a lesson in fight, man.

The stars that are growing so fast on our flags,
    We treasure as Liberty's pearls,
And stainless we 'll bear them, though shot into
      rags ;
    They were fix'd by the hands of our girls.
And fixed stars they shall be in our national sky,
    To guide through the future aright, man,
And young Cousin Sam, with their gleam in his
      eye,
    May dare the whole world to fight, man.

[NOTE. — The foregoing lines were written on the 8th
of January, 1861, for a friend who had intended to sing

them in the theatre, but thought at the time to be too much in the secession spirit. "Cousin Sam," or C. S., Confederate States.] *Richmond Examiner.*

———◆———

LINCOLN'S INAUGURAL ADDRESS.

(IN ADVANCE OF ALL COMPETITORS.)

BY A " SOUTHERN RIGHTS " MAN.

I COME at the people's mad-jority call,
   To open the Nation's quarternary ball,
And invite black and white to fall into ranks,
To dance a State jig on Republican planks.

I 'll fiddle like Nero, when Rome was on fire,
And play any tune that the people desire.
So let us be merry, — whatever the clatter be, —
Whilst playing: " O dear! O me! what can the
     matter be ? "

I 've made a great speech for the people's diversion,
And talked about billet-doux, love, and coercion ;
Of the spot I was born, of the place I was reared,
And the girl that I kissed on account of my beard.

I 'll settle the tariff — there 's no one can doubt it,
But, as yet, I know nothing or little about it ;

And as for those Southerners' bluster and clatter,
I know very well that there 's nothing the matter.

You 've oft heard repeated those wonderful tales
Of my beating a giant in splitting up rails;
And ere I left home — you know the fact is true —
That I beat a small Giant at politics, too.

Should it now be the will of the NORTH and the
    FATES,
I can do it up BROWN, by the splitting of States;
And then, when the State-splitting business fails,
I 'll resume my old trade as a splitter of rails.

Baltimore Republican.

BALTIMORE, *April* 23, 1861.

THE CALL OF FREEDOM.

HARK ! to the rescue ! Freedom calls,
   Where triumph's banners brightly wave,
And triumphs he who nobly falls,
   For glory gilds his honored grave !
But fall he will not, if on high
   Still rules the Mighty and the Just,
Or, daring thus, if doom'd to die,
   The tyrant first shall bite the dust !

Virginia!   Queen of nations proud!
  How grand in all the classic past!
Thine offspring, Freedom, calls aloud,
  And Honor echoes back the blast!
The fame of all thine ancient years,
  The demigods of olden time,
Dispel the dastard dream of fears,
  And dare thee act thy part sublime.

Virginia answers to the call!
  Virginia, ever great and free :
The brave, the beautiful, and all
  From river to the rolling sea.
From mountain crag, and teeming vale,
  From every humble hamlet home,
As swift as sweeps the lightning gale,
  Her stalwart children, crowding, come!

They come! they come! devoutly fired,
  To do or die, in Freedom's cause ;
By justice armed, by God inspired,
  To vindicate their sovereign laws!
And Heaven will shield the honored breast
  That braves the tyrant's stripes unfurl'd,
And victory o'er that banner rest,
  Whose dawning splendors fill the world!

All proudly gleams the golden dawn, .
  The starred Aurora of the free ;
All brightly bursts the blazing morn
  Of fixed and faithful Liberty.
Forever flame that standard high
  O'er mountain crest and surging stream,
Where courage, faith, and purity,
  In loving lustres blending beam !

In Southern skies, on Southern soil,
  O'er honest Southern heads and hearts,
For all who think, for all who toil,
  Till life's last lingering drop departs,
Shall grandly wave in glory bright,
  From gulf to bay, from sea to sea,
In one undying blaze of light,
  That noblest ensign of the free.

By all that woman's love inspires,
  By all that breathes above the sod,
By the fond ashes of our sires,
  By the eternal truth of God,
Where land the felons but to die,
  Their footsteps first shall be their last !
Their base-born blood shall shock the sky !
  And havoc shudder back aghast !

Hark ! to the rescue !   Freedom calls,
 Where Freedom's banners brightly wave,
And triumphs he who nobly falls,
 For glory gilds his honored grave !
But fall he will not, if on high
 Still rules the Mighty and the Just,
Or, daring thus, if doom'd to die,
 The tyrant first shall bite the dust !
  Richmond, *May* 1, 1861.

———◆———

MANASSAS.

BY A REBEL.

UPON our country's border lay,
 Holding the ruthless foe at bay,
Through chilly night and burning day,
  Our army at Manassas.

To them our eager eyes were turned,
While many a restless spirit burned,
And many a fond heart wildly yearned,
  O'er loved ones at Manassas.

For fast the Vandals gathered, strong
In wealth and numbers, all along

Our highways pressed a countless throng,
      To battle at Manassas.

With martial pomp and proud array,
With burnished arms and banners gay,
Panting for the inhuman fray,
      They rolled upon Manassas.

The opening cannons' thunders rent
The air, and ere their charge was spent,
Muskets and rifles quickly sent
      Death to us at Manassas.

But, like a wall of granite, stood
The true, the great, the brave, the good,
Who, firmly holding field and wood,
      Guarded us at Manassas.

They promptly answered fire with fire;
Danger could not with fear inspire
Their hearts, whose courage rose the higher,
      When death ruled at Manassas.

At dawn the murderous work begun;
The battle fiercely raged at noon;
Evening drew on, — 't was not done, —
      The carnage at Manassas.

Oh, trembling Freedom ! didst thou stay
Throughout that agonizing day,
To watch where victory would lay
      Her laurels at Manassas ?

Yea ! and thy potent trumpet tone
Ordered our gallant warriors on,
To the bold charge which for thee won
      The triumph at Manassas.

Well might the dastard foemen yield,
When Right and Vengeance joined to wield
The well-aimed ball and glittering steel,
      Which hurled them from Manassas.

They broke, and fear lent wings to feet
Flying before our chargers fleet,
Which followed up their wild retreat, —
      Their mad rout at Manassas.

Strike ! Southrons, strike ! for ne'er a foe
So worthy of your every blow
Can your good swords and carbines know,
      As those who sought Manassas.

For that our homes are still secure,
Our wives and sisters still left pure,

Our altars drip not with our gore ;
       Thanks, victors of Manassas !

Thy charmed trumpet sound, O Fame !
Let music catch the loud refrain,
While in a glad, triumphant strain,
       We celebrate Manassas.

And every soldier's breast shall fire
With emulation, and desire
To equal — fame can point no higher —
       The heroes of Manassas.

Alas ! that many writhe in pain,
Whose precious blood was spilt to gain
Glory and freedom on thy plain, —
       Thy bloody plain, Manassas.

If sympathy can aught avail,
If fervent prayers with Heaven prevail,
In your behalf they shall not fail,
       Poor wounded of Manassas.

Alas ! that blended with the tone
Of triumph, breathes the stifled moan
For many brave, whose dear lives won
       The victory of Manassas.

A grateful nation long shall keep
Their memory, and flock to weep
Above the turf where softly sleep
        The martyrs of Manassas.
HANOVER CO., *Va.*, *July* 30.

————◆————

CHIVALROUS C. S. A.

BY " B."

AIR —"*Vive la Compagnie!*"

I 'LL sing you a song of the South's sunny clime,
        Chivalrous C. S. A.!
Which went to house-keeping once on a time;
        Bully for C. S. A.!
Like heroes and princes they lived for awhile,
        Chivalrous C. S. A.!
And routed the Hessians in most gallant style;
        Bully for C. S. A.!
Chorus — Chivalrous, chivalrous people are they!
        Chivalrous, chivalrous people are they!
        In C. S. A.! In C. S. A.!
        Aye, in chivalrous C. S. A.!

They have a bold leader — Jeff. Davis his name —
        Chivalrous C. S. A.!

Good generals and soldiers, all anxious for fame;
    Bully for C. S. A.!
At Manassas they met the North in its pride,
    Chivalrous C. S. A.!
But they easily put McDowell aside;
    Bully for C. S. A.!
  Chorus — Chivalrous, chivalrous people, &c.

Ministers to England and France, it appears,
    Have gone from the C. S. A.!
Who 've given the North many fleas in its ears;
    Bully for C. S. A.!
Reminders are being to Washington sent,
    By the chivalrous C. S. A.!
That 'll force Uncle Abe full soon to repent;
    Bully for C. S. A.!
  Chorus — Chivalrous, chivalrous people, &c.

Oh, they have the finest of musical ears,
    Chivalrous C. S. A.!
Yankee Doodle 's too vulgar for them, it appears;
    Bully for C. S. A.!
The North may sing it and whistle it still,
    Miserable U. S. A.!
Three cheers for the South! — now, boys, with a
    will!
    And groans for the U. S. A.!
  Chorus — Chivalrous, chivalrous people, &c.

BATTLE ODE TO VIRGINIA.

OLD Virginia! virgin-crowned
   Daughter of the royal Bess,
Send the fiery ensign round,
Call your chivalry renowned, —
   Lineage of the lioness.

You have thrown the gauntlet down,
   Pledged to vindicate the right;
Bid your sons from field and town,
Through summer's smile and winter's frown,
   Make ready for the fight.

Now that you have drawn the sword,
   Throw away the useless sheath;
Hear your destiny's award, —
Drive the invaders from your sward,
   Or lay your heads beneath.

In the field with conflict rife,
   None must falter, yield, or fly;
Honor, liberty, and life,
All are staked upon the strife;
   You must " do or die."

Let your daughters shed no tear,
   Though their dearest may be slain;

None for *self* must hope or fear,
All with joy their burdens bear,
  Till you are free again.

By the consecrated soil
  Where your Washington had birth,
Keep your homes from ruthless spoil,
Keep your shield from spot or soil,
  Or perish from the earth.

—◆—

THE BATTLE-FIELD OF MANASSAS.

BY M. F. BIGNEY.

FILL, fill the trump of fame
  With the name —
Manassas, — the battle-field of pride ; —
Where Freedom's heroes fought with their spirits
    all a-flame,
Where the Gospel of Liberty was sounded with ac-
    claim,
  Where heroes for Liberty have died !

Come, Fancy, once again
Fill the plain with armed men ;
Let us see the struggling hosts of Wrong and Right ;
  Let the tide of battle pour,

Fight and conquer o'er and o'er,
Till we glow with inspiration at the sight.

There 's glory in the air :
    Everywhere
Glory rises from the ground,
    All around.
A hundred thousand men,
Gather in from hill and glen,
And for battle fierce and bloody they are bound.

See, see the cohorts come,
To the sound of fife and drum ;
They 're the foemen of the North
    Coming forth,
In the pride of conscious might ;
They would trample down the Right,
As forth they come, those foemen of the North.

The flag which they bear
    Is a snare :
Its Stripes writhe as snakes upon the air ;
And its Stars, no longer bright,
Tell of chaos and of night,
    And of how they yet
      Will set
      In despair.

On comes the lengthening line,
   As if eager for the wine
Which from the press of battle freely flows;
   And from the Southern heart
   Such wine will freely start,
As the pledge to each hecatomb of foes.

On comes the lengthened line,
   And a " higher law " *divine;*
The snakes on their banners seem to hiss;
   " Destruction to the South,"
   Bursts in hate from every mouth,
And the demon-words are held akin to bliss.

A brave, heroic band,
    Hand to hand,
To meet the shock of battle are prepared;
   For wife and child they stand, —
   For home and native land; —
Oh, pray that every hero may be spared!

The drum and fife may sound,
   But their stirring notes are drowned
In the roar and the thunder of the guns;
   The death-charged bullets fly,
   And the shells ascend the sky —
They are offerings to God's and Freedom's sons.

Where Freedom nerves the arm,
    There 's a charm ;
Where Freedom stirs the heart,
    Fears depart.
Oh, sacred is the strife,
And the sacrifice of life,
Where Freedom's chosen heroes point the dart.

God ! how the freemen press !
    There 's distress
In each lead and iron shower that they send ;
    Their countless columns pour,
    Like the waves in wild uproar,
    Beating on a rocky shore
        They would rend.

But firm as rocks our band
    Grandly stand, —
For home and native land
    Hand to hand.
How the proud invaders reel,
As with shot and shell and steel,
Destruction wide we deal,
    Sternly grand !

Again, and yet again,
These wild, fanatic men, —

Those foemen that invade our Southern homes, —
　　Still rally to the cry :
　　" We must conquer here, or die !
The laurel, or the fate of hellish gnomes ! "

　　Again, and yet again,
　　　　Southern men
Force the fierce insulting foe to retire.
　　Again the Northmen fall,
　　And to Heaven vainly call,
　　　　While they yell,
　　　" There is hell
In Southern fire ! "

Speed, Beauregard the brave, onward speed !
Speed, Davis unto Johnson, in his need !
　　Hurrah ! the foemen fly !
　　Send the victor shout on high,
For Heaven still rewards the daring deed.

　　How fearfully they bleed, —
　　　　Man and steed !
　　Oh, how their dying prayer
　　　　Rends the air !
　　All this for Northern greed,
　　And that strange, fanatic creed,

Which so wickedly they heed.
    Do not spare !

"The Southron is accurst,"—
    So they say ;
" He 's baser than the worst
    Beast of prey ; "
And the African is white,
In those Northern foemen's sight,
As the lily, when it greets the god of day.

Then drive them to their lair ;
    Do not spare !
Let shot and shell reply
    To their cry.
Though their bodies taint the air,
And become the vulture's fare,
It is just that such invading hordes should die.

McDowell, in the van,
Sees his beaten columns fly !
    He calls on God and man
    For the aid that both deny ;
The army he would rally, as it runs.
    Thus, thus McDowell raves :
" Know ye not, ye unworthy knaves,

That you fight the fight for slaves —
    Sable ones;
Come, and purchase redder graves
    With your guns."

But the guns are thrown away,
The invaders will not stay;
To them a fearful lesson has been read:
    For miles strewn all around,
    Encrimsoning the rich ground,
Lie their fallen friends, — the wounded and the
        dead.

The sun slopes down the west,
But the foe in wild unrest
Rushes on, though destruction follows fast.
    The Southern cavalcade
    Dyes with red each trusty blade,
And the carnage is terrible and vast!

Oh, where is Scott, the chief?
Why brings he not relief?
And Patterson, the tardy, where is he?
    And where is Abe, the Great,
    With his cap and cloak of state?
        He should see
How his warriors can flee.

Fear lendeth speed to flight,
And the foe invokes the night
To let its starless curtain quickly fall ;
But it falleth all too slow,
For the terrors of the foe,
And it seems to them the shadow of a pall.

A Nemesis concealed
In the shades of wold and field,
Breathes of vengeance to the foemen as they run ;
They are rushing in despair,
But there 's carnage everywhere,
And they know not what to welcome or to shun.

Ten thousand of their slain
Strew the plain ;
The shrieks from ten thousand more arise ;
And the ghosts
From their hosts
Wail despairingly and vain,
In their pain,
For a welcome to the skies.

At morning, in their pride,
Side by side,
They went forth in their might
To the fight ;

And now they flee in fear,
Trembling like the stricken deer,
At the sabre and the spear —
    It is night.

They came forth to destroy,
With a fierce, fanatic joy,
And boasted of the Rebels they would slay;
    But, ere the set of sun,
There are hundreds chased by one,
And they pray their legs to bear them safe
    away.

For miles strewn all around
    O'er the ground,
The records of their flight
    Meet the sight:
Bodies 'neath the horses' tread;
Bodies living; bodies dead;
And the swords and guns most beautifully bright!

But let us leave the foe
    In their woe.
To the God of Peace and Battle let us go.
    Let us praise the King of Kings,
    'Neath whose wide-expanded wings
There is shelter for his children here below.

His arm, unseen, uprears
    Freedom's spears ;
If Freedom's voice be weak,
    His will speak
In the cannon's thunder tones,
Though the answer be in groans,
And though a thousand tyrant hearts may break.

FLIGHT OF DOODLES.

I COME from old Manassas, with a pocket full
    of fun —
I killed forty Yankees with a single-barrelled
    gun ;
It don't make a niff-a-stifference to neither you
    nor I,
Big Yankee, Little Yankee, all run or die.

I saw all the Yankees at Bull Run,
They fought like the devil when the battle first
    begun.
But it don't make a niff-a-stifference to neither you
    nor I,
They took to their heels, boys, and you ought to
    see 'em fly.

I saw old Fuss-and-Feathers Scott, twenty miles
    away,
His horses stuck up their ears, and you ought to
    hear 'em neigh;
But it don't make a niff-a-stifference to neither you
    nor I,
Old Scott fled like the devil, boys; root, hog, or
    die.

I then saw a " Tiger," from the old Crescent
    City,
He cut down the Yankees without any pity;
Oh! it don't make a diff-a-bitterence to neither you
    nor I,
We whipped the Yankee boys, and made the
    boobies cry.

I saw South Carolina, the first in the cause,
Shake the dirty Yankees till she broke all their
    jaws;
Oh! it don't make a niff-a-stifference to neither you
    nor I,
South Carolina give 'em ——, boys; root, hog, or
    die.

I saw old Virginia, standing firm and true,
She fought mighty hard to whip the dirty crew;

Oh! it don't make a niff-a-stiffcrence to neither
     you nor I,
Old Virginia 's blood and thunder, boys ; root, hog,
     or die.

I saw old Georgia, the next in the van,
She cut down the Yankees almost to a man ;
Oh! it don't make a niff-a-stifference to neither
     you nor I,
Georgia 's sum in a fight, boys ; root, hog, or die.

I saw Alabama in the midst of the storm,
She stood like a giant in the contest so warm ;
Oh! it don't make a niff-a-stifference to neither
     you nor I,
Alabama fought the Yankees, boys, till the last one
     did fly.

I saw Texas go in with a smile,
But I tell you what it is, she made the Yankees bile ;
Oh! it don't make a niff-a-stifference to neither
     you nor I,
Texas is the devil, boys ; root, hog, or die.

I saw North Carolina in the deepest of the battle,
She knocked down the Yankees and made their
     bones rattle ;

Oh! it don't make a niff-a-stifference to neither
    you nor I,
North Carolina's got the grit, boys; root, hog, or
    die.

Old Florida came in with a terrible shout,
She frightened all the Yankees till their eyes stuck
    out;
Oh! it don't make a niff-a-stifference to neither
    you nor I,
Florida's death on Yankees; root, hog, or die.

CONFEDERATE SONG.

Air — "*Bruce's Address.*"

Written for and dedicated to the Kirk's Ferry Rangers,
by their Captain, E. Lloyd Wailes. Sung by the Glee
Club on the 4th of July, 1861, at the Kirk's Ferry bar-
becue, (Catahoula, La.,) after the presentation of a
flag, by the ladies, to the Kirk's Ferry Rangers.

RALLY round our country's flag!
    Rally, boys, nor do not lag;
Come from every vale and crag,
    Sons of Liberty!

Northern Vandals tread our soil,
Forth they come for blood and spoil,
To the homes we 've gained with toil,
　　Shouting, " Slavery ! "

Traitorous Lincoln's bloody band
Now invades the freeman's land,
Arm'd with sword and firebrand,
　　'Gainst the brave and free.

Arm ye, then, for fray and fight,
March ye forth both day and night,
Stop not till the foe 's in sight,
　　Sons of chivalry.

In your veins the blood still flows
Of brave men who once arose —
Burst the shackles of their foes;
　　Honest men and free.

Rise, then, in your power and might,
Seek the spoiler, brave the fight;
Strike for God, for Truth, for Right :
　　Strike for Liberty !

DESTRUCTION OF THE VANDAL HOST AT MANASSAS.

A PARODY.

APE Lincoln came down like a wolf on the fold,
And his cohorts were thirsting for silver and
gold;
Though the sheen of their swords was like stars on
the sea,
Yet it saved not their life-stream which crimsoned
the lea.

Like the hordes of the forest, when the war-whoop
is heard,
These serfs came by stealth on the braves whom
they feared;
Like the leaves of the forest, when autumn hath
blown,
These cowards their backs to the brave ones hath
shown.

For our cannon and ball, spreading wide o'er the
blast,
Carried death to the foe — sparing few as they
passed;

And the eyes of the Vandals waxed deadly and
    chill,
And our soil is now drenched by their vile crimson
    rill !

And there stood old Scott, sad, dejected, and pale,
When he heard from the hireling the heart-rend-
    ing tale ;
Beside him, the dying, — their wounds gaping wide,
In an instant to be like the dead by their side.

All hushed into silence, the dying alone
Interrupt the death-calm by a heart-breaking moan ;
And the blood of the slain cries aloud to the Lord,
For his vials of wrath on the prince of the horde.

And the wives of the Vandals are heard in their
    wail
With high imprecations Ape Lincoln to hail ;
And the Saracen's might, yet untouched by our
    sword,
Shall share the same fate, for our trust's in the
    Lord.   J. J. H.

SOUTHERN SONG.

Tune — "*Wait for the Wagon.*"

COME, all ye sons of freedom,
  And join our Southern band,
We are going to fight the Yankees,
  And drive them from our land.
Justice is our motto,
  And Providence our guide,
So jump into the wagon,
  And we 'll all take a ride.
      Chorus — So wait for the wagon ! the dis-
        solution wagon ;
      The South is the wagon, and we 'll all take
        a ride.

Secession is our watchword ;
  Our rights we all demand ;
To defend our homes and firesides
  We pledge our hearts and hands.
Jeff. Davis is our President,
  With Stephens by his side ;
Great Beauregard our General ;
  He joins us in our ride.
      Chorus — Wait for the wagon, &c.

Our wagon is the very best ;
  The running gear is good ;
Stuffed round the sides with cotton,
  And made of Southern wood.
Carolina is the driver,
  With Georgia by her side ;
Virginia holds the flag up,
  While we all take a ride.
    Chorus — Wait for the wagon, &c.

The invading tribe, called Yankees,
  With Lincoln for their guide,
Tried to keep Kentucky
  From joining in the ride ;
But she heeded not their entreaties, —
  She has come into the ring ;
She would n't fight for a government
  Where cotton was n't king.
    Chorus — So wait for the wagon, &c.

Old Lincoln and his Congressmen,
  With Seward by his side,
Put old Scott in the wagon,
  Just for to take a ride.
McDowell was the driver,
  To cross Bull Run he tried,

But there he left the wagon
  For Beauregard to ride.
    Chorus — Wait for the wagon, &c.

Manassas was the battle-ground ;
  The field was fair and wide ;
The Yankees thought they 'd whip us out,
  And on to Richmond ride ;
But when they met our " Dixie " boys,
  Their danger they espied ;
They wheeled about for Washington,
  And didn't wait to ride.
    Chorus — So wait for the wagon, &c.

Brave Beauregard, God bless him !
  Led legions in his stead,
While Johnson seized the colors
  And waved them o'er his head.
To rising generations,
  With pleasure we will tell
How bravely our Fisher
  And gallant Johnson fell.
    Chorus — So wait for the wagon, &c.

                    Raleigh Register.

SONG FOR THE IRISH BRIGADE.

NOT now for the songs of a nation's wrongs,
  Nor the groans of starving labor;
Let the rifle ring and the bullet sing
  To the clash of the flashing sabre!
There are Irish ranks on the tented banks
  Of Columbia's guarded ocean;
And an iron clank, from flank to flank,
  Tells of armèd men in motion.

And the frank souls there, clear, true, and bare
  To all, as the steel beside them,
Can love or hate, with the strength of Fate,
  Till the grave of the valiant hide them.
Each seems to be mailed *Ard Righ*,
  Whose sword's avenging glory
Might light the fight and smite for Right,
  Like Brian's in olden story!

With pale affright and panic flight
  Shall dastard Yankees, base and hollow,
Hear a Celtic race, from their battle place,
  Charge to the shout of " *Faugh-a-ballagh!* "
By the souls above, by the land we love,
  Her tears and bleeding patience,
The sledge is wrought that shall smash to naught
  The brazen liar of nations.

The Irish green shall again be seen
  As our Irish fathers bore it,
A burning wind from the South behind,
  And the Yankee rout before it !
O'Neil's red hand shall purge the land —
  Rain fire on men and cattle,
Till the Lincoln snakes in their own cold lakes
  Plunge from the blaze of battle.

The knaves that rest on Columbia's breast,
  And the voice of true men stifle,
We 'll exorcise from the rescued prize —
  Our talisman, the rifle ;
For a tyrant's life a bowie-knife ! —
  Of Union-knot dissolvers,
The best we ken are stalwart men,
  Columbiads and revolvers !

Whoe'er shall march by triumphal arch,
  Whoe'er may swell the slaughter,
Our drums shall roll from the capitol
  O'er Potomac's fateful water !
Rise, bleeding ghosts, to the Lord of Hosts,
  For judgment final and solemn ;
Your fanatic horde to the edge of the sword
  Is doomed, line, square, and column.

SHAMROCK,
Sumpter Rifles.

7

YANKEE VANDALS.

Air — "*Gay and Happy.*"

THE Northern Abolition vandals,
  Who have come to free the slave,
Will meet their doom in " Old Virginny,"
Where they all will get a grave.
Chorus. So let the Yankees say what they will,
    We 'll love and fight for Dixie still,
    Love and fight for, love and fight for,
    We 'll love and fight for Dixie still.

They started for Manassas Junction,
With an army full of fight,
But they caught a Southern tartar,
And they took a bully flight.
    So let the Yankees, etc.

" Old Fuss-and-Feathers " could not save them,
All their boasting was in vain,
Before the Southern steel they cowered,
And their bodies strewed the plain.
    So let the Yankees, etc.

The " Maryland Line " was there as ever,
With their battle-shout and blade,

They shed new lustre on their mother,
When that final charge they made.
    So let the Yankees, etc.

Old Abe may make another effort
For to take his onward way,
But his legions then as ever,
Will be forced to run away.
    So let the Yankees, etc.

Brave Jeff. and glorious Beauregard,
With dashing Johnston, noble, true,
Will meet their hireling hosts again,
And scatter them like morning dew.
    So let the Yankees, etc.

When the Hessian horde is driven,
O'er Potomac's classic flood,
The pulses of a new-born freedom,
Then will stir old Maryland's blood.
    So let the Yankees, etc.

From the lofty Alleghanies,
To old Worcester's sea-washed shore,
Her sons will come to greet the victors,
There in good old Baltimore.
    So let the Yankees, etc.

Then with voices light and gladsome,
We will swell the choral strain,
Telling that our dear old mother,
Glorious Maryland 's free again.
    So let the Yankees, etc.

Then we 'll crown our warrior chieftains,
Who have led us in the fight,
And have brought the South in triumph,
Through dread danger's troubled night.
    So let the Yankees, etc.

And the brave who nobly perished,
Struggling in the bloody fray,
We 'll weave a wreath of fadeless laurel
For their glorious memory.
    So let the Yankees, etc.

O'er their graves the Southern maidens,
From sea-shore to mountain grot,
Will plant the smiling rose of beauty,
And the sweet forget-me-not.
    So let the Yankees, etc.

THE SOUTH IS UP.

BY P. E. C.

THE South is up in stern array —
   Chasseurs and Zouaves and Gallic Guard —
Types of their veteran fathers gray,
   Of war-mark'd visage, sabre-scarr'd —
The children of Marengo's plains,
   Of Austerlitz and Waterloo,
When tyrants dare to speak of chains
   We 'll do as their brave sires would do.
The sturdy German, hardy Pole,
   Who knows how Kosciusko fell —
The Tyrolean, who feels his soul
   Fired with that spark which gave them Tell.

The South is up ! Italia's sons —
   A Garibaldi in each form —
Their hands are grasping freemen's guns,
   Their bosoms feel his valor warm ;
Their crimson shirts, in bloody fields,
   Like walls of flame shall front the foeman ;
In that dread hour whoever yields,
   'T is not the offspring of the Roman ;
No renegade, to scorn his brother
While guarding their adopted mother —

One feeling *nationale* and grand
Still binds them to their native land.

The South is up ! those brawny hands
  That bless in peace or crush in war,
Who fought on India's burning sands
  At Egypt's Nile, and Trafalgar ;
That reckless mirth, that fiery joy,
  On field, or fort, or slippery deck,
From Clontarf's plains to Fontenoy,
  At Quatre Bras or old Quebec ;
Magenta, Malakoff, Redan,
  Has heard their Celtic " Clear the way ! "
The slandered, exiled Irishman
  Stands for his Southern home to-day ;
And when, perchance, in Death's eclipse
  He grasps her flag with 'legiance due,
The last breath lingering on his lips
  Might proudly say, I 'm Irish, too !

The South is up ! her native sons,
  Whose spirit prompts them to be free,
Spring forth to man their trophied guns,
  So bravely won at Monterey —
Surpassing Buena Vista's deeds,
  Or Palo Alto's feats again,
Though wives be wreathed in widows' weeds

And children weep for fathers slain.
What! think to bind the South? 'T is vain!
  Freedom's inheritors at birth —
Not all the leagued infernal train,
  If they were mustered here on earth,
Those flashing eyes, like gleaming steel,
  Those hero boys and veterans gray!
Oh, yes! the throbbing heart can feel —
  The South is up in stern array.

Yet sad 't will grieve the Southern heart
  To meet their brethren foot to foot,
But cancers on a vital part
  Must now be severed branch and root;
They share with us a blood-bought fame
  From foreign foe and savage grim;
The memory of our George's name,
  Revered by us, is dear to them;
Our ships in every clime have shown,
  Where jealous monarchies might see,
What stars upon our flag have grown
  From old *thirteen* to *thirty-three;*
Soldier to lead, or sage to teach,
  Deep-scienced minds, of knowledge vast,
The great one's fame, as in a niche,
  Lives in the history of the past.
Now, pausing o'er our doubtful fate
  We *have been,* or we *shall be,* great.

THE OLD RIFLEMAN.

BY FRANK TICKNOR, M. D.

NOW, bring me out my buckskin suit!
　　My pouch and powder, too!
We 'll see if seventy-six can shoot
　　As sixteen used to do.

Old Bess! we 've kept our barrels bright!
　　Our triggers quick and true!
As far, if not as *fine* a sight,
　　As long ago, we drew!

And pick me out a trusty flint!
　　A real white and blue;
Perhaps 't will win the *other* tint,
　　Before the hunt is through!

Give boys your brass percussion-caps!
　　Old " shut-pan " suits as well!
There 's something in the *sparks;* perhaps
　　There 's something in the smell!

We 've seen the red-coat Briton bleed!
　　The red-skin Indian, too!
We never thought to draw a bead
　　On Yankee-doodle-doo!

But, Bessie! bless your dear old heart!
　　Those days are mostly done;
And now we must revive the art
　　Of shooting on the run!

If Doodle must be meddling, why,
　　There 's only this to do:
Select the black spot in his eye
　　And let the daylight through!

And if he does n't like the way
　　That Bess presents the view,
He 'll, maybe, change his mind and stay
　　Where the good Doodles do!

Where Lincoln lives.　The man, you know,
　　Who kissed the Testament;
To keep the Constitution?　No!
　　To keep the Government!

We 'll hunt for Lincoln, Bess! old tool,
　　And take him half and half;
We 'll aim to *hit* him, if a fool,
　　And *miss* him if a calf!

We 'll teach these shot-gun boys the tricks
　　By which a war is won;

Especially how seventy-six
Took Tories on the run.

———◆———

THE SOUTHERN CROSS.

FLING wide each fold, brave flag, unrolled
  In all thy breadth and length!
Float out unfurled, and show the world
  A new-born nation's strength.
Thou dost not wave all bright and brave
  In holiday attire;
'Mid cannon chimes a thousand times
  Baptized in blood and fire.

No silken toy to flaunt in joy,
  When careless shouts are heard:
Where thou art borne all scathed and torn,
  A nation's heart is stirred.
Where half-clad groups of toil-worn troops
  Are marching to the wars,
What grateful tears and heartfelt cheers
  Salute thy cross of stars!

Thou ne'er hast seen the pomp and sheen,
  The pageant of a court;
Or masquerade of war's parade,
  When fields are fought in sport:

But thou know'st well the battle yell
  From which thy foemen reel,
When down the steeps resistless leaps
  A sea of Southern steel.

Thou know'st the storm of balls that swarm
  In dense and hurtling flight,
When thy crossed bars, a blaze of stars,
  Plunge headlong through the fight :
Where thou 'rt unfurled are thickest hurled
  The thunderbolts of war ;
And thou art met with loudest threat
  Of cannon from afar.

For thee is told the merchant's gold :
  The planter's harvests fall :
Thine is the gain of hand and brain,
  And the heart's wealth of all.
For thee each heart has borne to part
  With what it holds most dear ;
Through all the land no woman's hand
  Has staid one volunteer.

Though from thy birth outlawed on earth,
  By older nations spurned,
Their full-grown fame may dread the name
  Thy infancy has earned.

For thou dost flood the land with blood,
  And sweep the seas with fire;
And all the earth applauds the worth
  Of deeds thou dost inspire!

Thy stainless field shall empire wield,
  Supreme from sea to sea,
And proudly shine the honored sign
  Of peoples yet to be.
When thou shalt grace the hard-won place
  The nations grudge thee now,
No land shall show to friend or foe
  A nobler flag than thou.

———◆———

UP! UP! LET THE STARS OF OUR BANNER.

BY M. F. BIGNEY.

RESPECTFULLY DEDICATED TO THE SOLDIERS OF THE SOUTH.

UP! up! Let the stars of our banner
  Flash out like the brilliants above;
Beneath them we'll shield from dishonor
  The homes and the dear ones we love.
    With " God and our Right!"
    Our cry in the fight,
    We'll drive the invader afar,

And we 'll carve out a name
In the temple of Fame
With the weapons of glorious war.

Arise with an earnest endeavor —
A nation shall hallow the deed ;
The foe must be silenced forever,
Though millions in battle may bleed.
With " God and our Right ! " etc.

Strong arms and a conquerless spirit
We bring as our glory and guard :
If courage a triumph can merit,
Then Freedom shall be our reward.
With " God and our Right ! " etc.

Beneath the high sanction of Heaven,
We 'll fight as our forefathers fought ;
Then pray that to us may be given
Such guerdon as fell to their lot.
With " God and our Right ! " etc.

HURRAH!

BY A MISSISSIPPIAN.

HURRAH ! for the Southern Confederate State,
With her banner of white, red, and blue ;

Hurrah! for her daughters, the fairest on earth,
  And her sons, ever loyal and true!

Hurrah! and hurrah! for her brave Volunteers,
  Enlisted for freedom or death;
Hurrah! for Jeff. Davis, Commander-in-Chief,
  And three cheers for the Palmetto wreath!

Hurrah! for each heart that is right in the cause;
  That cause we 'll protect with our lives;
Hurrah! for the first one who dies on the field,
  And hurrah! for each one who survives!

Hurrah! for the South — shout hurrah! and hur-
  rah !
O'er her soil shall no tyrant have sway.
In peace or in war we will ever be found
  "Invincible," now and for aye.

Mobile Register.

THE SOLDIER BOY.

BY H. M. L.

I GIVE my soldier boy a blade,
  In fair Damascus fashioned well;
Who first the glittering falchion swayed,
  Who first beneath its fury fell,

I know not : but I hope to know
   That for no mean or hireling trade,
To guard no feeling, base or low,
   I give my soldier boy a blade.

Cool, calm, and clear, the lucid flood,
   In which its tempering work was done ;
As calm, as clear, as clear of mood
   Be thou whene'er it sees the sun ;
For country's claim, at honor's call,
   For outraged friend, insulted maid,
At mercy's voice to bid it fall,
   I give my soldier boy a blade.

The eye which marked its peerless edge,
   The hand that weigh'd its balanced poise,
Anvil and pincers, forge and wedge,
   Are gone with all their flame and noise ;
And still the gleaming sword remains.
   So when in dust I low am laid,
Remember by these heartfelt strains,
   I give my soldier boy a blade.
       Lynchburg, *May* 18, 1861.

A SOUTHERN GATHERING SONG.

BY L. VIRGINIA FRENCH.

Air — *"Hail Columbia."* *

SONS of the South, beware the foe !
    Hark to the murmur deep and low,
Rolling up like the coming storm,
Swelling up like sounding storm,
Hoarse as the hurricanes that brood
In space's far infinitude !
Minute guns of omen boom
Through the future's folded gloom ;
Sounds prophetic fill the air,
Heed the warning — and prepare !
    Watch ! be wary — every hour
    Mark the foeman's gathering power —
    Keep watch and ward upon his track
    And crush the rash invader back !

Sons of the brave ! — a barrier stanch
Breasting the alien avalanche —

* A good clergyman, on being censured for introducing
a "song tune" into his choir at church, replied that he
"did not think it fair that the Devil should have all the
good music." In like manner, we will *never* give up
"Hail Columbia" to the Abolitionists. It is *ours;* and
we mean to hold, as one of our dearest rights, this, the
grandest march ever composed by mortal man.

Manning the battlements of RIGHT ;
Up, for your *Country, "God, and right !"*
Form your battalions steadily,
And strike for death or victory !
Surging onward sweeps the wave,
Serried columns of the brave,
Banded 'neath the benison
Of Freedom's godlike Washington !
  Stand ! but should the invading foe
  Aspire to lay your altars low,
    Charge on the tyrant ere he gain
    Your iron arteried domain !

Sons of the brave ! when tumult trod
The tide of revolution — God
Looked from His throne on "the things of time,"
And two new stars in the reign of time
He bade to burn in the azure dome —
The freeman's LOVE and the freeman's HOME !
Holy of Holies ! guard them well,
Baffle the despot's secret spell,
And let the chords of life be riven
Ere you yield those gifts of Heaven !
  Io pœan ! trumpet notes
  Shake the air where our banner floats ;
  Io triumphe ! still we see
  The land of the South is the home of the free !
8

BATTLE-CALL.

Nec temere, nec timide.

DEDICATED TO HER COUNTRYMEN, THE CAVALIERS OF THE SOUTH,

BY ANNIE CHAMBERS KETCHUM.

GENTLEMEN of the South!
 Gird on your flashing swords!
Darkly along your borders fair
 Gather the ruffian hordes!
Ruthless and fierce they come;
 Even at the cannon's mouth
To blast the glory of your land,
 Gentlemen of the South!

Ride forth in your stately pride,
 Each bearing on his shield
Ensigns your fathers won of yore
 On many a well-fought field.
Let this be your battle-cry,
 Even to the cannon's mouth,
Cor unum via una! Onward!
 Gentlemen of the South!

Brave knights of a knightly race,
 Gordon and Chambers and Gray,

Show to the minions of the North
  How valor dares the fray !
Let them read on each spotless crest,
  Even at the cannon's mouth,
Decori decus addit avito,
  Gentlemen of the South !

Morrison, Douglas, Stuart,
  Erskine and Bradford and West,
Your gauntlets on many a hill and plain
  Have stood the battle's test.
Animo non astutia !
  March to the cannon's mouth,
Heirs of the brave dead centuries,
  Gentlemen of the South !

Call out your stalwart men,
  Workers in brass and steel,
Bid the swart artisans come forth
  At sound of the trumpet's peal ;
Give them your war-cry, Erskine,
  Fight to the cannon's mouth —
Bid the men *forward*, Douglas, forward !
  Yeomanry of the South !

Brave hunters, ye have met
  The fierce black bear in the fray,

Ye have trailed the panther night by night,
  Ye have chased the fox by day ;
Your prancing chargers pant
  To dash at the gray wolf's mouth,
Your arms are sure of their quarry — forward !
  Gentlemen of the South !

Fight ! that the lowly serf
  And the high-born lady, still
May bide in their proud dependency,
  Free subjects of your will ;
Teach the base North how ill —
  At the belching cannon's mouth —
He fares who touches your household gods,
  Gentlemen of the South !

From mother, and wife, and child,
  From faithful and happy slave,
Prayers for your sake ascend to Him
  Whose arm is strong to save.
We check the gathering tears,
  Though ye go to the cannon's mouth ;
Dominus providebit ! Onward !
  Gentlemen of the South !
      DUNROBIN COTTAGE.

ANOTHER YANKEE DOODLE.

YANKEE Doodle had a mind
  To whip the Southern traitors,
Because they did n't choose to live
  On codfish and potatoes.
    Yankee Doodle, doodle-doo,
      Yankee Doodle dandy,
    And so to keep his courage up
      He took a drink of brandy.

Yankee Doodle said he found
  By all the census figures,
That he could starve the rebels out,
  If he could steal their niggers.
    Yankee Doodle, doodle-doo,
      ·Yankee Doodle dandy,
    And then he took another drink
      Of gunpowder and brandy.

Yankee Doodle made a speech;
  ' T was very full of feeling:
I fear, says he, I cannot fight,
  But I am good at stealing.
    Yankee Doodle, doodle-doo,
      Yankee Doodle dandy,

Hurrah for Lincoln, he 's the boy
To take a drop of brandy.

Yankee Doodle drew his sword,
And practised all the passes;
Come, boys, we 'll take another drink
When we get to Manassas.
Yankee Doodle, doodle-doo,
Yankee Doodle dandy,
They never reached Manassas plain,
And never got the brandy.

Yankee Doodle soon found out
That Bull Run was no trifle;
For if the North knew how to steal,
The South knew how to rifle.
Yankee Doodle, doodle-doo,
Yankee Doodle dandy,
'T is very clear I took too much
Of that infernal brandy.

Yankee Doodle wheeled about,
And scampered off at full run,
And such a race was never seen
As that he made at Bull Run.
Yankee Doodle, doodle-doo,
Yankee Doodle dandy,

I hav n't time to stop just now
To take a drop of brandy.

Yankee Doodle, oh ! for shame,
You 're always intermeddling ;
Let guns alone, they 're dangerous things ;
You 'd better stick to peddling.
Yankee Doodle, doodle-doo,
Yankee Doodle dandy,
When next I go to Bully Run
I 'll throw away the brandy.

Yankee Doodle, you had ought
To be a little smarter ;
Instead of catching woolly heads,
I vow you 've caught a tartar.
Yankee Doodle, doodle-doo,
Yankee Doodle dandy,
Go to hum, you 've had enough
Of rebels and of brandy.

THE BONNIE BLUE FLAG.

WE are a band of brothers, and natives to the
  soil,
Fighting for the property we gained by honest toil
And when our rights were threatened, the cry rose
  near and far :
Hurrah for the bonnie Blue Flag that bears a
  single star !
Chorus — Hurrah ! hurrah ! for the bonnie Blue
  Flag
  That bears a single star.

As long as the Union was faithful to her trust,
Like friends and like brothers, kind were we and
  just ;
But now when Northern treachery attempts our
  rights to mar,
We hoist on high the bonnie Blue Flag that bears
  a single star.

First, gallant South Carolina nobly made the stand ;
Then came Alabama, who took her by the hand ;
Next, quickly, Mississippi, Georgia, and Florida —
All raised the flag, the bonnie Blue Flag that
  bears a single star.

Ye men of valor, gather round the banner of the
　　right;
Texas and fair Louisiana join us in the fight.
Davis, our loved President, and Stephens, states-
　　men are;
Now rally round the bonnie Blue Flag that bears
　　a single star.

And here's to brave Virginia! the Old Dominion
　　State
With the young Confederacy at length has linked
　　her fate.
Impelled by her example, now other States prepare
To hoist on high the bonnie Blue Flag that bears
　　a single star.

Then here's to our Confederacy; strong we are
　　and brave,
Like patriots of old we'll fight, our heritage to save;
And rather than submit to shame, to die we would
　　prefer;
So cheer for the bonnie Blue Flag that bears a
　　single star.

Then cheer, boys, cheer, raise the joyous shout,
For Arkansas and North Carolina now have both
　　gone out;

And let another rousing cheer for Tennessee be
　　given,
The 'single star of the bonnie Blue Flag has
　　grown to be eleven !

THE BATTLE AT BULL RUN.

BY RUTH.

FORWARD, my brave columns, forward !
　　No other word was spoken ;
But in the quick and mighty rustling of their feet,
And in the flashing of their eyes, 't was proved
This was enough.
Men, whose *every* bosom held a *noble* heart,
And who had left their homes, their sacred *rights*
To gain : To *these* this was no trying hour,
No time to waver, and to doubt.　But one,
For which they 'd hoped and prayed —
One (as they felt) they 'd brought not on
Themselves, but which they knew *must come* —
And *nobly, O most nobly*, did their
Bravery, their *sense* of *right*, sustain them.

And Lincoln's hordes —
They knew *not* with what natures they contended,

Seemed not to feel their *motives* differed, as
Does heaven from earth.
They, the poor, miserable, *hired* outcasts, whose
Principles were bought,
And men, whose courage, bravery, and noble aims,
Had come to be, throughout the land,
A proverb.

And *what* the end ?
What *could*, what *should it be*, than what it *was ?*
A *brilliant, glorious* VICTORY.

The South weeps o'er her slain :
And well she may ; for they were jewels
From her diadem.
She weeps ; sheds tears of grief, of sorrow,
And of PRIDE.

  LOUISVILLE, Ky., *July* 24, 1861.

THE SOUTHRON MOTHER'S CHARGE.

BY THOMAS B. HOOD.

YOU go, my son, to the battle-field,
 To repel the invading foe ;

Mid its fiercest conflicts *never* yield
   Till death shall lay you low.

Our God, who smiles upon the Right
   And frowns upon the Wrong,
Will nerve you for our holy fight,
   And make your courage strong.

Our cause is just, for it we pray
   At morning, noon, and night,
Upon our banners we inscribe,
   God, Liberty, and Right.

I love you as I love my life,
   You are my only son ;
Your country calls, go forth and fight
   Till Freedom's cause is won.

It may be that you fall in death,
   Contending for your home,
Yet your aged mother will not be
   Forsaken though alone.

A thousand generous hearts there are
   Throughout this sunny land,
Whose ample fortunes will be spent
   With an unsparing hand.

Now, go, my son, a mother's prayers
  Will ever follow thee ;
And in the thickest of the fight
  Strike home for liberty !

On every hill, in every glen,
  We 'll fight till we are free ;
We 'll fight till every limpid brook
  Runs crimson to the sea.

No truce we know, till every foe
  Shall leave our hallowed sod,
And we regain that heaven-born boon,
  " Freedom to worship God."
New Orleans, La.

A CALL TO KENTUCKIANS.

BY A SOUTHERN RIGHTS WOMAN.

SONS of Kentucky ! arise from your dreaming !
  Awake, and to arms ! for the foe draweth nigh ;
Must ye wait till our land with their legions are
    teeming
  Ere ye rise in your might to battle or die ?

Oh, list to the wail from Missouri's heart coming,
  As trampled and bleeding she shrinks from the
    foe;
Oh, such is our fate if thus ye lie sleeping;
  Then wake from your slumbers and shield us
    from woe.

The spirits of those who in battle have fallen
  Are weeping in shame at your cowardly fear;
The watchword of fiends hath already been given
  To crush and destroy all your loved ones so
    dear.

Has the day gone fore'er when 't were nobler to be
  A son of Kentucky than diadems wear?
Be ye cowards and slaves? Are ye no longer
    free?
  That thus with your traitorous tyrants ye bear!

Then rise in your might and repel each invader,
  Nor let our loved land be disgraced by their
    tread;
Let the watchword be " Freedom and States Rights
    forever! "
  Nor cease till each foe shall lie low with the
    dead.

LOUISVILLE, KY., *June 24, 1861.*

THE STARS AND BARS.

'TIS sixty-two!—and sixty-one,
 With the old Union, now is gone,
  Reeking with bloody wars—
Gone with that ensign, once so prized,
The Stars and Stripes, now so despised,
  Struck for the Stars and Bars.

The burden once of patriot's song,
Now badge of tyranny and wrong,
  For us no more it waves;
We claim the stars—the stripes we yield,
We give *them* up on every field,
  Where fight the Southern braves.

Our motto this,—" God and our Right;"
For sacred liberty we fight—
  Not for the lust of power;
Compelled by wrongs the sword t' unsheath,
We 'll fight, be free, or cease to breathe—
  We 'll die before we cower.

By all the blood our fathers shed,
We will from tyranny be freed—
  We will not conquered be;

Like them, no higher power we own
But God's — we bow to Him alone —
    We will, we will be free!

For homes and altars we contend,
Assured that God will us defend —
    He makes our cause His own;
Not of our gallant patriot host,
Not of brave leaders do we boast —
    We trust in God alone.

Sumter, and Bethel, and Bull Run
Witnessed fierce battles fought and won,
    By aid of Power Divine;
We met the foe, who us defied,
In all his pomp, in all his pride,
    Shouting: " Manasseh's mine !".

It was not thine, thou boasting foe !
We laid thy vandal legions low —
    We made them bite the sod ;
At Lexington the braggart yields,
Leesburgh, Belmont, and other fields ; —
    Still help us, mighty God !

Thou smiledst on the patriot seven —
Thou smilest on the brave eleven

Free, independent States;
Their number Thou wilt soon increase,
And bless them with a lasting peace,
Within their happy gates.

No more shall violence then be heard,
Wasting destruction no more feared
In all this Southern land;
" Praise," she her gates devoutly calls,
" Salvation," her heaven-guarded walls —
What shall her power withstand?

" The little one," by heavenly aid,
" A thousand is — the small one made,
" A nation — oh! how strong!"
Jehovah, who the right befriends,
Jehovah, who our flag defends,
Is hastening it along!

———◆———

KING SCARE.

THE monarch that reigns in the *warlike* North,
    Aint Lincoln at all I ween,
But old King Scare, with his thin, fast legs,
    And his long sword in between;

The world has not for many a day
　　Seen merrier king or lord;
But some declare, in a playful way,
　　Scare should not wear a sword.
　　　　Yes, I have heard, upon my word,
　　　　　　And seen in prose and rhyme,
　　　　That if old Scare no sword would wear,
　　　　　　He 'd make much better time.

I cannot tell why he put it on,
　　Nor tell where he got the heart,
But guess he intended it all for fun,
　　And not for a tragedy part;
But well made up with his togs and wear,
　　With his boots and sword and gun,
Not one of us knew it was old King Scare,
　　Till we saw the monarch run.
　　　　It did us good, to see him scud
　　　　　　And put the miles behind him;
　　　　His friends now say, " put your sword away,"
　　　　　　But old Scare does n't mind 'em.

He is ruler of twenty terrible States,
　　With ships and soldiers and tin;
But the state that all of these out-rates
　　Is the terrible state he is in;
With just nowhere for his ships to move,

With his tin most terribly rare,
With his soldiers on every field to prove
True subjects of old King Scare.
The English " Times " and " Punch " in rhymes
Both say the *Republic 's nil*,
That after the war, just as before
Scare will be despot still.

Scare rides a horse in his " own countrie,"
And a high horse rides King Scare,
And a mighty host in his train there be
Who nor gun nor falchion wear ;
Now, these be the freedom-shriekers bold
Who keep off the war-'gine's track,
Who shut on the white race dungeon doors,
And send " braves " to steal the black.
For Abolition is but a mission
Of white-skinned niggers, to pray,
And steal, and make the blacks they take
As free and as mean as they.

This monarch Scare is imperious quite,
And he loves to swear and chafe
At the " rebel " foe that, in every fight,
He can always run from — safe ;
And all his gazettes in great round words
His " brave volunteers " bepraise,

Whom Scare drives up against "rebel" swords,
  And the swords drive otherways.
    Thus into battle, driven like cattle,
      Come his "brave volunteers;"
    Then from the fight, with all their might,
      Each gallantly — disappears.

Hurrah for the land of old Scare, then;
  Hurrah for the Yankee land!
What a proud old war were this if their men
  Could only be made to stand;
How the guns would roar, and the steel would ring,
  And the souls up to heaven would flare,
If all the Yankees had now for king
  Old Courage, and not old Scare.
    But never they that lie and pray
      And steal and murder too,
    Have pluck to fight, for only the Right
      Is the soldier to dare and do.

New Orleans, *October* 16, 1861.

OUR BRAVES IN VIRGINIA.

Air — *"Dixie Land."*

WE have ridden from the brave Southwest,
  On fiery steeds, with throbbing breast;

Hurrah ! hurrah ! hurrah ! hurrah !
With sabre flash and rifle true, —
Hurrah ! hurrah ! —
The Northern ranks we will cut through,
And charge for Old Virginia, boys.
Hurrah ! hurrah !
Then charge for Old Virginia.

We have come from the cloud-capp'd mountains,
From the land of purest fountains;
Hurrah ! hurrah ! hurrah ! hurrah !
Our sweethearts and wives conjure us, —
Hurrah ! hurrah ! —
Not to leave a foe before us,
And strike for Old Virginia, boys, &c.

Then we 'll rally to the bugle call;
For Southern rights we 'll fight and fall;
Hurrah ! hurrah ! hurrah ! hurrah !
Our gray-haired sires sternly say, —
Hurrah ! hurrah !
That we must die or win the day.
Three cheers for Old Virginia, boys, &c.

Then our silken banner wave on high;
For Southern homes we 'll fight and die.
Hurrah ! hurrah ! hurrah ! hurrah !

Our cause is right, our quarrel just, —
    Hurrah! hurrah!
We 'll in the God of battles trust,
    And conquer for Virginia, boys, &c.

----♦----

FROM THE SOUTH TO THE NORTH.

BY C. L. S.

THERE is no union when the hearts
    That once were bound together
Have felt the stroke that coldly parts
    All kindly ties forever.
Then oh! your cruel hands draw back,
    And let us be divided
In peace, since it is proved we lack
    The grace to live united.

We cannot bear your scorn and pride,
    Your malice and your taunting,
That have for years our patience tried —
    Your hypocritic canting.
We WILL not bow our necks beneath
    The yoke that you decree us,

We WILL be free, though only death
  Should have the power to free us!

Oh, Southern sons are bold to dare,
  And Southern hearts courageous.
Nor meekly will they longer bear
  Oppression so outrageous.
And you shall feel our honest wrath,
  If hearts so cold *can* feel;
Shall meet us in your Southern path
  And prove our Southern steel.

We ask no favor at your hand,
  No gifts and no affection;
But only peace upon our land,
  And none of your protection.
We ask you now, henceforth, to know
  We are a separate nation;
And be assured we 'll fully show
  We scorn your " proclamation."

We were not first to break the peace,
  That blessed our happy land;
We loved the quiet, calm, and ease,
  Too well to raise a hand,
Till fierce oppression stronger grew,
  And bitter were your sneers —

Then to our land we must be true,
  Or show a coward's fears !

We loved our banner while it waved
  An emblem of our Union,
The fiercest danger we had braved
  To guard that sweet communion.
But when it proved that " stripes " alone,
  Were for our sunny South,
And all the " stars " in triumph shone
  Above the chilly North, —

Then, not till then, our voices rose
  In one tumultuous wave —
We WILL the tyranny oppose,
  Or find a bloody grave !
Another flag shall lead our hosts
  To battle on the plain,
The " rebels " will defy your boasts,
  And prove your sneering vain !

There is no danger we could fear, —
  No hardship or privation, —
To free the land we hold so dear,
  From tyrannous dictation.
Blockade her ports, — her seas shall swell
  Beneath your ships of war,

And every breeze in anger tell
  Your tyranny afar.

Her wealth may fail — her commerce droop
  With every foreign nation ;
But mark you, if her pride shall stoop,
  Or her determination !
The products of her fields will be
  For food and raiment too, —
From mountain cliff to rolling sea
  Her children will be true.

Her banner may not always wave
  On victory's fickle breath,
The young, the chivalrous, and brave,
  May feel the hand of death.
But, when her gallant sons have died,
  Her daughters will remain —
Nor crushed will be the Southern pride,
  Till they too, all are slain.

———◆———

MY DREAM.

LO ! in my dream, I saw the dove
  Just hovering o'er the troubled sea,

With the olive-branch of peace and love —
  Sweet emblem of the change to be.

Our nation now by war disturbed,
  Will soon on quiet laurels rest;
Confederate armies, long perturbed,
  Return with " victor " on each crest.

Our nation's foes will be disarmed,
  Be wearied of disastrous war ;
I saw it, — yes, my soul was charmed —
  In dreams, I saw the dove, not far.

Oh, haste ! then haste the happy day
  That brings to us a sweet release
From clamor, turmoil, dread affray,
  And all that breaks a nation's peace.

EAST BATON ROUGE, *Nov.* 7, 1861.   L. F——.

THE SONG OF THE EXILE.

AIR — *"Dixie."*

OH ! here I am in the land of cotton,
  The flag once honored is now forgotten ;
Fight away, fight away, fight away for Dixie's
  land.

But here I stand for Dixie dear,
To fight for freedom, without fear ;
   Fight away, fight away, fight away for Dixie's
      land.
    Chorus. For Dixie's land I'll take my stand,
          To live or die for Dixie's land.
          Fight away, fight away, fight away for
            Dixie's land.

Oh ! have you heard the latest news,
Of Lincoln and his kangaroos ;
   Fight away, etc.
His minions they would now oppress us,
With war and bloodshed they 'd distress us !
   Fight away, etc.

Abe Lincoln tore through Baltimore,
In a baggage-car with fastened door ;
   Fight away, etc.
And left his wife, alas ! alack !
To perish on the railroad track !
   Fight away, etc.

Abe Lincoln is the President,
He 'll wish his days in Springfield spent ;
   Fight away, etc.
We 'll show him that old Scott 's a fool,

We 'll ne'er submit to Yankee rule!
  Fight away, etc.

At first our States were only seven,
But now we number stars eleven;
  Fight away, etc.
Brave old Missouri shall be ours,
Despite old Lincoln's Northern powers!
  Fight away, etc.

We have no ships, we have no navies,
But mighty faith in the great Jeff. Davis;
  Fight away, etc.
Due honor, too, we will award
To gallant Bragg and Beauregard!
  Fight away, etc.

Abe's proclamation in a twinkle,
Stirred up the blood of Rip Van Winkle;
  Fight away, etc.
Jeff. Davis's answer was short and curt:
" Fort Sumter 's taken, and ' nobody 's hurt!' "
  Fight away, etc.

We hear the words of this same ditty,
To the right and left of. the Mississippi;
  Fight away, etc.

In the land of flowers, hot and sandy,
From Delaware Bay to the Rio Grande !
   Fight away, etc.

The ladies cheer with heart and hand,
The men who fight for Dixie's land;
   Fight away, etc.
The " Stars and Bars " are waving o'er us,
And Independence is before us !
   Fight away, etc.

MARTINSBURG, Va.

THE MARCH.

BY JOHN W. OVERALL.

TRAMP, tramp, tramp, tramp !
   Go the Southern braves to battle,
How they shine, each gleaming line !
   Flashing sabres ! how they rattle !
Every lip is now compress'd,
   Every heart now yearns for glory,
Every eye with patriot fire
   Burns for battle fierce and gory !

Tramp, tramp, tramp, tramp !
   Death is in each hidden sabre,

Reaper of the fields of Time,
  Look ye for a giant's labor!
How sublime! when patriots feel
  All the strength of self-reliance,
Marching on to meet the foe,
  With a stern and grim defiance!

See how proudly floats our flag!
  White! our cause is pure and grand, man!
Red! a living flood shall flow
  From every foe now in the land, man!
Blue! aye, heaven's stars are there!
  Sparkling in their azure beauty!
Tramp, tramp, tramp, tramp!
  Go the messengers of duty!

SOUTHERN WAR SONG.

BY N. P. W.

TO horse! to horse! our standard flies,
  The bugles sound the call;
An alien navy stems our seas —
The voice of battle 's on the breeze,
  Arouse ye, one and all!

From beauteous Southern homes we come,
  A band of brothers true —
Resolved to fight for liberty,
And live or perish with our flag —
  The noble Red and Blue.

Though tamely crouch to Northern frown,
  Kentucky's tardy train;
Though invaded soil Maryland mourns,
Though brave Missouri vainly spurns,
  And foaming gnaws the chain;

Oh! had they marked the avenging call
  Their brethren's insults gave,
Disunion ne'er their ranks had mown,
Nor patriot valor, desperate grown,
  Sought freedom in the grave!

Shall we, too, bend the stubborn head,
  In freedom's temple born —
Dress our pale cheek in timid smiles,
To hail a master in our house,
  Or brook a victor's scorn?

No! though destruction o'er the land
  Come pouring as a flood,
The sun that sees our falling day,

Shall mark our sabre's deadly sway,
  And set that night in blood !

For gold let Northern legions fight,
  Or plunder's bloody gain ;
Unbribed, unbought, our swords we draw,
To guard our homes, to fence our law,
  Nor shall their edge be vain.

And now that breath of Northern gale
  Has fanned the Stars and Bars,
And footstep of invader rude,
With rapine foul, and red with blood,
  Us rights and liberty debars.

Then farewell home, and farewell friends,
  Adieu each tender tie,
Resolved we mingle in the tide,
Where charging squadrons furious ride,
  To conquer or to die.

To horse, to horse ! the sabres gleam,
  High sounds our bugle-call,
Combined by honor's sacred tie,
Our word is, Rights and Liberty !
  March forward, one and all !

Louisville Courier.

WE 'LL BE FREE IN MARYLAND.

BY ROBERT E. HOLTZ.

Air — "*Gideon's Band.*"

THE boys down South in Dixie's land,
　The boys down South in Dixie's land,
The boys down South in Dixie's land,
Will come and rescue Maryland.
Chorus — If you will join the Dixie band,
　　　Here 's my heart and here 's my hand,
　　　If you will join the Dixie band;
　　　We 're fighting for a home.

The Northern foes have trod us down,
The Northern foes have trod us down,
The Northern foes have trod us down,
But we will rise with true renown.
　　If you will join the Dixie band, etc.

The tyrants they must leave our door,
The tyrants they must leave our door,
The tyrants they must leave our door,
Then we 'll be free in Baltimore.
　　If you will join the Dixie band, etc.
10

These hirelings they 'll never stand,
These hirelings they 'll never stand,
These hirelings they 'll never stand,
Whenever they see the Southern band.
    If you will join the Dixie band, etc.

Old Abe has got into a trap,
Old Abe has got into a trap,
Old Abe has got into a trap,
And he can't get out with his Scotch cap.
    If you will join the Dixie band, etc.

Nobody 's hurt is easy spun,
Nobody 's hurt is easy spun,
Nobody 's hurt is easy spun,
But the Yankees caught it at Bull Run.
    If you will join the Dixie band, etc.

We rally to Jeff. Davis true,
Beauregard and Johnston, too,
Magruder, Price, and General Bragg,
And give three cheers for the Southern flag.
    If you will join the Dixie band, etc.

We 'll drink this toast to one and all,
Keep cocked and primed for the Southern call;

The day will come, we 'll make the stand,
Then we 'll be free in Maryland.
　　If you will join the Dixie band, etc.
January 30, 1862.

———◆———

WAR SONG.

BY J. H. WOODCOCK.

TUNE — *"Bonnie Blue Flag."*

HUZZA ! huzza ! let 's raisé the battle-cry,
　　And whip the Yankees from our land,
Or with them fall and die.
　　Rush on our Southron columns,
And make the brigands feel
　　That all the booty they will get,
Will be our Southron steel.
　　Huzza ! huzza ! let 's raise (the) our banner
　　　　high,
And nobly drive the Yankees out,
　　Or with them fall and die.

Rush on the columns — let every Southron brave
　　Nobly charge the accursed foe,
Or find a soldier's grave.
　　With bowie and with pike,

We 'll rally to the field,
   And bravely to the last we 'll strike,
Resolved we 'll never yield.
   Huzza ! huzza ! etc.

We are fighting for our mothers, our sisters, and our
       wives ;
   For these, and our country's rights,
We 'll sacrifice our lives.
   Then, trusting still to Heaven,
We 'll charge th' invading host,
   Till liberty and independence
Shall be the nation's boast.
   Huzza ! huzza ! etc.

Then on with our columns — slay the vandal foe —
   Beat them from our sunny soil,
And lay their colors low.
   To the great God of nations
Our sacred cause confide,
   For we are fighting for our liberty,
And He is on our side.
   Huzza ! huzza ! etc.

A NEW RED, WHITE, AND BLUE.

WRITTEN FOR A LADY, BY JEFF. THOMPSON.

MISSOURI is the pride of the nation,
    'The hope of the brave and the free ;
The Confederacy will furnish the rations,
But the fighting is trusted to thee ;
For, brave boys, your soil has been noted,
And your flag has been trusted to you ;
For freedom you have not yet voted,
But you fight for the Red, White, and Blue.
    Chorus — Three cheers, &c.

The Stars shall shine bright in the heaven
But the Stripes should be trailed in the dust,
For they are no longer the sign of the haven
Of the brave, of the free, or the just ;
The Bars now in triumph shall wave
O'er the land of the faithful and true ;
O'er the home of the Southern brave,
Shall float the new Red, White, and Blue.
    Chorus — Three cheers, &c.

O JOHNNY BULL, MY JO JOHN.

Air — *"John Anderson, my Jo."*

It was stated in the *Richmond Dispatch* during the last days of December, 1861, that a gentleman, just from the West Indies, had said that there were eighty-seven British ships-of-war lying in those waters. This statement gave rise to the following imitation of an old song : —

O JOHNNY Bull, my Jo John! I wonder what you mean,
By sending all these frigates out, commissioned by the Queen ;
You 'll frighten off the Yankees, John, and why should you do so ?
Best catch and sink, or burn them all, O Johnny Bull, my Jo !

O Johnny Bull, my Jo John ! when Yankee hands profane,
Were laid in wanton insult upon the lion's mane,
He roared so loud and long, John, they quickly let him go,
And sank upon their trembling knees, O Johnny Bull, my Jo !

O Johnny Bull, my Jo John! when Lincoln first
    began
To try his hand at war, John, you were a peaceful
    man ;
But now your blood is up, John, and well the
    Yankees know,
You play the ———— when you start, O Johnny
    Bull, my Jo !

O Johnny Bull, my Jo John, let 's take the field
    together,
And hunt the Yankee Doodles home, in spite of
    wind and weather,
And ere a twelvemonth roll around, to Boston we
    will go,
And eat our Christmas dinner there, O Johnny
    Bull, my Jo !

"SOUTHRONS."

YOU can never win them back —
    Never ! never !
Though they perish on the track
    Of your endeavor ;
Though their corses strew the earth,

That SMILED upon their birth,
And blood pollutes each hearth-
    Stone forever!

They have risen to a man,
    Stern and fearless;
Of your curses and your ban
    They are careless.
Every hand is on its knife,
Every gun is primed for strife,
Every PALM contains a life,
    High and peerless!

You have no such blood as theirs
    For the shedding:
In the veins of cavaliers
    Was its heading!
You have no such stately men
In your " abolition den,"
To march through foé and fen,
    Nothing dreading!

They may fall before the fire
    Of your legions,
Paid with gold for murderous hire —
    Bought allegiance;
But for every drop you shed,

You shall have a mound of dead,
So that vultures may be fed
    In our regions !

But the battle to the strong
        Is not given,
When the Judge of Right and Wrong
        Sits in heaven ;
And the God of David still
Guides the pebble with *His will ;*
There are giants yet to kill —
        Wrongs unshriven !

"These stirring verses, which we copy from a Southern exchange, are from the patriotic pen of a lady of Kentucky, who has achieved a national reputation as a poetess and authoress." — *Louisville Courier.*

———◆———

"NIL DESPERANDUM."

INSCRIBED TO OUR SOLDIER-BOYS,

BY ADA ROSE.

THE Yankee hosts are coming,
    With their glittering rows of steel
And sharp, from many a skirmish,
    Comes the rifle's ringing peal,

Warning you how very near
   The Northern " Hessians " are,
With their overwhelming forces ;
   But ne'er must you despair.

For though they come on, surging
   Like a mighty rolling sea,
They 're *hired* by their master, "Abe " —
   You fight for *Liberty.*
So bravely you must meet them,
   And face the cannon's blare ;
Your watchword, " Victory or Death,"
   And never you despair.

True, the cloud is dark and lowering,
   But behind a cheerful ray,
And the night is always darkest
   Just before the break of day.
Have faith ; the cloud will soon disperse,
   For the light is surely there ;
The day will soon be dawning,
   So never you despair.

Go, emulate brave Washington,
   Who led a little band,
To drive the proud oppressors
   From off their happy land.

The enemy outnumbered,
  By far, the " rebels " there;
But bravely they encountered them,
  Nor yielded to despair.

'T is said that " rebel " chieftain,
  Ere they sought the battle's fray,
Would ask our heavenly Father
  To be their shield and stay;
And then they 'd march with confidence,
  Well knowing He 'd be there;
And that must be the reason why
  They never did despair.

Likewise, if you will ask Him,
  He 'll meet you on the field,
To be a guard about you,
  And your support and shield;
The foe shall fly before you,
  As you shout your victory there;
Then don't forget to plead with Him,
  And never to despair.

      PINE BLUFF, Ark.

ADDRESS OF THE WOMEN TO THE SOUTHERN TROOPS.

BY MRS. J. T. H. CROSS.

AIR — *"Bruce's Address."*

SOUTHERN men, unsheathe the sword,
  Inland and along the board;
Backward drive the Northern horde —
  Rush to victory!

Let your banners kiss the sky,
Be " The Right " your battle cry!
Be the God of Battles nigh, —
  Crown you in the fight!

Pressing back the tears that start,
We behold your hosts depart;
Saying, with heroic heart,
  Clothe your arms with might!

Lower the proud oppressor's crest!
Or, if he should prove the best,
Dead, not dishonored, rest
  On the field of blood!

We — may God so give us grace! —
Sons will rear, to take your place;

Strong the foeman's steel to face —
    Strong in heart and hand!

Death your serried ranks may sweep,
Proud shall be the tears we weep —
Sacredly our hearts shall keep
    Memory of your deeds!

Though our land be left forlorn,
Spirit of the Southron-born
Northern rage shall laugh to scorn —
    Northern hosts defy.

He that last is doomed to die
Shall, with his expiring sigh,
Send aloft the battle-cry,
    " God defend the Right!"

—◆—

A NORTH CAROLINA CALL TO ARMS.

BY LUOLA.

Air — "*The Old North State.*"

YE sons of Carolina! awake from your dreaming!
   The minions of Lincoln upon us are streaming!
Oh! wait not for argument, call, or persuasion,

To meet at the onset this treach'rous invasion !
    Defend, defend the old North State forever ;
    Defend, defend the good old North State.

Oh ! think of the maidens, the wives, and the moth-
    ers ;
Fly ye to the rescue, sons, husbands, and brothers,
And sink in oblivion all party and section ;
Your hearth-stones are looking to you for protec-
    tion !
    Defend, defend the old North State forever,
        etc.

Her name stands the foremost in Liberty's story,
Oh ! tarnish not now her fame and her glory !
Your fathers, to save her, their swords bravely
    wielded,
And she never yet has to tyranny yielded.
    Defend, defend the old North State forever,
        etc.

The babe in its sweetness, the child in its beauty,
Unconsciously urge you to action and duty !
By all that is sacred, by all to you tender,
Your country adjures, arise and defend her !
    Defend, defend the old North State forever,
        etc.

The national eagle, above us now floating,
Will soon on the vitals of loved ones be gloating;
His talons will tear, and his beak will devour;
Oh! spurn ye his sway, and delay not an hour.
    Defend, defend the old North State forever,
        etc.

The Star-Spangled Banner, dishonored, is stream-
    ing
O'er bands of fanatics; their swords are now gleam-
    ing;
They thirst for the life-blood of those you most
    cherish;
With brave hearts and true, then, arouse, or they
    perish!
    Defend, defend the old North State forever,
        etc.

Round the flag of the South, oh! in thousands now
    rally,
For the hour 's departed when freemen may dally;
Your all is at stake; then go forth, and God speed
    you,
And onward to glory and victory lead you!
    Hurrah! hurrah! the old North State forever!
    Hurrah! hurrah! the good old North State.

A SOUTHERN WOMAN'S SONG.

STITCH, stitch, stitch,
  Little needle swiftly fly,
  Brightly glittering as you go ;
Every time that you pass by
  Warms my heart with pity's glow.
Dreams of comfort that will cheer,
Through winter's cold the Volunteer,
Dreams of courage you will bring,
Smile on me like flowers in spring.

  Stitch, stitch, stitch,
Swiftly little needle fly,
  Through this flannel, soft and warm ;
Though with cold the soldier sigh,
  This will sure keep out the storm.
Set the buttons close and tight
  Out to shut the winter's damp ;
There 'll be none to fix them right
  In the soldier's tented camp.

  Stitch, stitch, stitch ;
Ah, needle do not linger ;
  Close the thread, make firm the knot ;
There 'll be no dainty finger
  To arrange a seam forgot.

Though small and tiny you may be,
  Do all that you are able;
A *mouse* a lion once set free, —
  As says the pretty fable.

    Stitch, stitch, stitch,
Swiftly little needle glide,
  Thine 's a pleasant labor;
To clothe the soldier be thy pride,
  While he wields the sabre.
Ours are tireless hearts and hands;
  To Southern wives and mothers,
All who join our warlike bands
  Are our friends and brothers.

    Stitch, stitch, stitch,
Little needle swiftly fly,
  From the morning until eve,
As the moments pass thee by,
  These substantial comforts weave.
Busy thoughts are at our hearts —
  Thoughts of hopeful cheer,
As we toil till day departs
  For the noble Volunteer.

    Quick, quick, quick,
Swifter little needle go;

From our homes' most pleasant fires
Let a loving greeting flow
To our brothers and our sires;
We have tears for those who fall, —
Smiles for those who laugh at fear, —
Hope and sympathy for all, —
Every noble Volunteer.

A WAR SONG FOR VIRGINIA.

SOUND, Virginia, sound your clarion!
From your serried ranks of war!
Fall in line with State of Marion,
And your glittering falchion draw!

Onward, onward, then to battle!
For bright Freedom points the way;
Though the grape-shot thickly rattle,
Onward, onward, to the fray!

Though each Northern squadron dashes
On, as wave up to the rock —
Though each foeman's sword-blade flashes,
Onward, onward, meet the shock!

Love of freedom, honor, glory,
   Makes each freeman's arm a host;
This we are taught by minstrel story, —
   Tyrants learn but at their cost.

Look, and see " proud Edward's power "
   Crushed by Bruce at Bannockburn;
See of Austria's host the flower
   Bite the dust by Lake Lucerne.

Mark the Persian hordes parading,
   Rushing, flee from Marathon !
And the British lion invading,
   Crouching to your Washington.

So, Virginia, sound your clarion !
   From your serried ranks of war !
Fall in line with State of Marion,
   And your glittering falchion draw !

For the banner which once floated
   Over Freedom's native land —
Flag, to which you are devoted,
   Is borne by a tyrant's band.

Save, oh, save it from pollution !
   Though your noblest sons fall dead;

Save it, though in revolution
  All its stars with blood be red!

Then, with " Southern Cross" emblazon
  Its blue field in colors bold,
So that we may proudly gaze on
  Fifteen clustering stars of gold.

LAND OF KING COTTON.

BY JO. AUGUSTINE SIGNAIGO.

Air — *" Red, White, and Blue."*

OH! Dixie, the land of King Cotton,
  The home of the brave and the free;
A nation by Freedom begotten,
  The terror of despots to be;
Wherever thy banner is streaming,
  Base tyranny quails at thy feet,
And Liberty's sunlight is beaming,
  In splendor of majesty sweet.
Chorus — Three cheers for our army so true,
  Three cheers for Price, Johnston, and Lee,
  Beauregard, and our Davis, forever;
  The pride of the brave and the free!

When Liberty sounds her war-rattle,
  Demanding her right and her due,
The first land who rallies to battle
  Is Dixie, the shrine of the true;
Thick as leaves of the forest in summer,
  Her brave sons will rise on each plain;
And then strike, until each vandal comer
  Lies dead on the soil he would stain.
      Three cheers for our army, &c.

May the names of the dead, that we cherish,
  Fill memory's cup to the brim;
May the laurels they 've won never perish,
  Nor " star of their glory grow dim; "
May the States of the South never sever,
  But champions of freedom e'er be;
May they flourish, Confed'rate forever,
  The boast of the brave and the free.
      Three cheers for our army, &c.

SONG FOR THE SOUTH.

OF all the mighty nations, in the East or in the
    West,
Our glorious Southern nation is the greatest and
    the best;

We have room for all true Southrons, with our
    Stars and Bars unfurled,
And a general invitation to the people of the
    world.
  Chorus — Then, to arms, boys! to arms, boys!
    make no delay,
Come from every Southern State, come from
    every way;
Our army is n't large enough; Jeff. Davis calls
    for " more,"
To hurl the vile invader from off our Southern
    shore.

Ohio is our northern line, far as her waters flow,
And on the south is the Rio Grande and the Gulf
    of Mexico;
While between the Atlantic Ocean, where the sun
    begins to rise,
Westward to Arizona, the land of promise lies.
    Then, to arms, boys! &c.

While the Gulf States raise the cotton, the others
    grain and pork,
North and South Carolina's factories will do the
    finer work;
For the deep and flowing waterfalls that course
    along our hills,

Are " just the things " for washing sheep and
　　driving cotton-mills.
　　　　Then, to arms, boys ! &c.

While the North is in commotion, and her " mon-
　　arch 's " in a fret,
We 're teaching them a lesson which they never
　　will forget ;
And this they fast are learning, that Dixie 's not a
　　fool,
For the men will do their fighting, while the chil-
　　dren go to school.
　　　　Then, to arms, boys ! &c.

Our Southern boys are brave and true, and are
　　joining heart and hand,
And are flocking to the Stars and Bars, as they are
　　floating o'er our land ;
And all are standing ready, with their rifles in
　　their hand,
And invite the North to open graves down South
　　in Dixie's land.
　　　　Then, to arms, boys ! &c.

THE FEDERAL VANDALS.*

THEY come, they come — a motley crew,
  For rapine, rape, and plunder met;
From different realms, of every hue,
  The olive, yellow, white, and jet,
The princely loom-lord, and his servile loot;
By sea and land they come, on horse, on foot.

Ye Southern freemen, who is he,
  By foes encompassed as thou art,
That will, that can deliver thee ?
  That dares attempt to take thy part ?
Hark ye ! in loudest thunder from on high,
The great Jehovah answers — " It is I."

Rise, then, ye freemen, old and young,
  Unsheathe your swords — be bold, be brave !
Away be every scabbard flung,
  In Federal blood your broadswords lave ;

* The writer has taken the liberty to vary and apply to
our Northern foes parts of an original poem in manuscript,
written by himself.

Arise, " arise and thresh " —'t is God's command,*
And sweep Abe's cringing minions from your land.

SENEX.

THE GUERILLAS.

AWAKE and to horse, my brothers!
    For the dawn is glimmering gray,
And hark! in the crackling brushwood
    There are feet that tread this way.

" Who cometh ? " " A friend." " What tidings ? "
    " O God! I sicken to tell ;
For the earth seems earth no longer,
    And its sights are sights of hell !

" From the far-off conquered cities
    Comes a voice of stifled wail,
And the shrieks and moans of the houseless
    Ring out, like a dirge on the gale.

* Micah iv. 13: "Arise and thresh, O daughter of Zion;
for I will make thine horn iron, and I will make thy hoof
brass, and thou shalt beat in pieces many people; and I
will consecrate their gain unto the Lord, and their sub-
stance unto the Lord of the whole earth."

"I 've seen from the smoking village
  Our mothers and daughters fly ;
I 've seen where the little children
  Sank down in the furrows to die.

" On the banks of the battle-stained river
  I stood as the moonlight shone,
And it glared on the face of my brother,
  As the sad wave swept him on.

" Where my home was glad, are ashes,
  And horrors and shame had been there,
For I found on the fallen lintel,
  This tress of my wife's torn hair !

" They are turning the slaves upon us,
  And with more than the fiend's worst art,
Have uncovered the fire of the savage,
  That slept in his untaught heart !

" The ties to our hearths that bound him,
  They have rent with curses away,
And maddened him, with their madness,
  To be almost as brutal as they.

" With halter, and torch, and Bible,
  And hymns to the sound of the drum,

They preach the gospel of murder,
    And pray for lust's kingdom to come.

" To saddle ! to saddle ! my brothers !
    Look up to the rising sun,
And ask of the God who shines there,
    Whether deeds like these shall be done !

" Wherever the vandal cometh,
    Press home to his heart with your steel,
And when at his bosom you cannot,
    Like the serpent, go strike at his heel.

" Through thicket and wood, go hunt him,
    Creep up to his camp-fire side,
And let ten of his corpses blacken,
    Where one of our brothers hath died.

" In his fainting, foot-sore marches,
    In his flight from the stricken fray,
In the snare of the lonely ambush,
    The debts we owe him, pay.

" In God's hand alone is vengeance,
    But he strikes with the hands of men,
And his blight would wither our manhood,
    If we smite not the smiter again.

" By the graves where our fathers slumber,
    By the shrines where our mothers prayed,
By our homes, and hopes, and freedom,
    Let every man swear on his blade,

" That he will not sheathe nor stay it,
    Till from point to hilt it glow
With the flush of Almighty vengeance,
    In the blood of the felon foe."

They swore — and the answering sunlight
    Leaped red from their lifted swords,
And the hate in their hearts made echo
    To the wrath in their burning words.

There 's weeping in all New England,
    And by Schuylkill's banks a knell,
And the widows there and the orphans,
    How the oath was kept, can tell.*

* It may add something to the interest with which
these stirring lines will be read, to know that they were
composed within the walls of a Yankee Bastile. They
reach us in manuscript, through the courtesy of a returned
prisoner. — *Richmond Examiner.*

A WELCOME TO THE INVADER.

"AN ODE,"

ADDRESSED TO THE PICKED MEN OF COL. WILSON'S NEW YORK
COMMAND.

I.

WHAT! have ye come to spoil our fields,
    Black hearts and bloody hands!
And taste the sweets that conquest yields
    To those who win our lands?

II.

Back to your dens of crime and shame,
    Black hearts and bloody hands!
Ye but disgrace a soldier's name,
    Owning such vile commands.

III.

Your ribald chieftain is a fool,
    Black hearts and bloody hands!
In sneaky Seward's grasp a tool
    In Blair's — a beast he stands.

IV.

Dare ye with patriot men to strive?
    Black hearts and bloody hands!

And can ye hope to 'scape alive
　From their avenging brands?

v.

Thieves, ruffians, hirelings, slaves,
　Black hearts and bloody hands!
Our country will refuse its graves
　To your polluted bands.

VI.

The carrion vulture in his flight,
　Black hearts and bloody hands!
Shall scent you, as you droop in fight,
　Nor wait your ebbing sands.

Charleston Courier.

LAND OF THE SOUTH.

BY A. F. LEONARD.

AIR — "*Friend of my Soul.*"

LAND of the South! the fairest land
　Beneath Columbia's sky!
Proudly her hills of freedom stand,
　Her plains in beauty lie.

Her dotted fields, her traversed streams
  Their annual wealth renew.
Land of the South! in brightest dreams
  No dearer spot we view.

Men of the South! a free-born race,
  They vouch a patriot line;
Ready the foeman's van to face,
  And guard their country's shrine.
By sire and son a haloing light
  Through time is borne along —
They " nothing ask but what is right,
  And yield to nothing wrong."

Fair of the South! rare beauty's crown
  Ye wear with matchless grace;
No classic fair of old renown
  Deserve a higher place.
Your vestal robes alike become
  The palace and the cot;
Wives, mothers, daughters! every home
  Ye make a cherished spot.

Flag of the South! aye, fling its folds
  Upon the kindred breeze;
Emblem of dread to tyrant holds —
  Of freedom on the seas.

Forever may its stars and stripes
  In cloudless glory wave;
Red, white, and blue — eternal types
  Of nations free and brave!

States of the South! the patriot's boast!
  Here equal laws have sway;
Nor tyrant lord, nor despot host,
  Upon the weak may prey.
Then let them rule from sea to sea,
  And crown the queenly isle —
Union of love and liberty,
  'Neath Heaven's approving smile!

God of the South! protect this land
  From false and open foes!
Guided by Thine all-ruling hand,
  In vain will hate oppose.
So mote the ship of State move on
  Upon the unfathomed sea;
Gallantly o'er its surges borne,
  The bulwark of the free.

THE STARS AND BARS.

BY A. J. REQUIER.

FLING wide the dauntless banner
   To every Southern breeze,
Baptized in flame, with Sumter's name —
A patriot and a hero's fame —
   From Moultrie to the seas!
That it may cleave the morning sun
   And, streaming, sweep the night,
The emblem of a battle won
   With Yankee ships in sight.

Come, hucksters, from your markets,
   Come, bigots, from your caves,
Come, venal spies, with brazen lies
Bewildering your deluded eyes,
   That we may dig your graves;
Come, creatures of a sordid clown
   And drivelling traitor's breath,
A single blast shall blow you down
   Upon the fields of Death.

The very flag you carry
   Caught its reflected grace,
In fierce alarms, from Southern arms,

When foemen threatened all your farms,
  And never saw your face ;
Ho ! braggarts of New England's shore,
  Back to your hills and delve
The soil whose craven sons foreswore
  The flag in eighteen-twelve !

We wreathed around the roses
  It wears before the world,
And made it bright with storied light,
In every scene of bloody fight
  Where it has been unfurled ;
And think ye, now, the dastard hands
  That never yet could hold
Its staff, shall wave it o'er our lands,
  To glut the greed of gold ?

No ! by the truth of Heaven
  And its eternal Sun,
By every sire whose altar fire
Burns on to beckon and inspire,
  It never shall be done ;
Before that day the kites shall wheel
  Hail-thick on Northern heights,
And there our bared, aggressive steel
  Shall countersign our rights !

Then, spread the flaming banner
  O'er mountain, lake, and plain,
Before its bars, degraded Mars
Has kissed the dust with all his stars,
  And will be struck again ;
For could its triumph now be stayed
  By Hell's prevailing gates,
A sceptred Union would be made
  The grave of sovereign States.

NORTH CAROLINA'S WAR SONG.

Air — *"Annie Laurie."*

WE leave our pleasant homesteads,
    We leave our smiling farms,
At the first call of duty
  We rush at once to arms,
  We rush at once to arms,
  To guard our coasts we fly,
For the land our mothers liv'd on
  Bravely to bleed or die.

Up, boys, and quit your pleasure,
  Up, men, and quit your toil !
The invader's foot must never

Be press'd upon our soil,
Be press'd upon our soil
In which our fathers sleep;
Their blessed graves our care, boys,
Most sacredly must keep.

'T was in our brave old State, men,
That first of all was sung,
The thrilling song of freedom
That through the land hath rung;
That through the land hath rung,
And we'll sound its notes once more
Till our men and children shout
From the mountains to the shore.

Sweet eyes are filled with tears, men,
Sweet tears of love and pride,
As our wives and sweethearts bid us
Go meet whate'er betide,
Go meet whate'er betide,
And God our guide shall be
As we drive the foe before us,
And rush to victory.

THERE'S LIFE IN THE OLD LAND YET!

BY JAS. R. RANDALL.

BY blue Patapsco's billowy dash,
    The tyrant's war-shout comes,
Along with the cymbal's fitful clash,
    And the growl of his sullen drums.
We hear it! we heed it, with vengeful thrills,
    And we shall not forgive or forget;
There's faith in the streams, there's hope in the
       hills,
    There's life in the old land yet!

Minions! we sleep, but we are not dead;
    We are crushed, we are scourged, we are
       scarred;
We crouch — 't is to welcome the triumph tread
    Of the peerless BEAUREGARD.
Then woe to your vile, polluting horde,
    When the Southern braves are met;
There's faith in the victor's stainless sword,
    There is life in the old land yet!

Bigots! ye quell not the valiant mind,
    With the clank of an iron chain,
The spirit of freedom sings in the wind,

O'er *Merryman*, *Thomas*, and *Kane*;
And we, though we smite not, are not thralls,
   Are piling a gory debt;
While down by McHenry's dungeon-walls,
   There's life in the old land yet!

Our women have hung their harps away,
   And they scowl on your brutal bands,
While the nimble poignard dares the day,
   In their dear defiant hands.
They will strip their tresses to string our bows,
   Ere the Northern sun is set;
There's faith in their unrelenting woes,
   There's life in the old land yet!

There's life, though it throbbeth in silent veins,
   'T is vocal without noise,
It gushed o'er Manassas's solemn plains,
   From the blood of the MARYLAND BOYS!
That blood shall cry aloud, and rise
   With an everlasting threat;
By the death of the brave, by the God in the
     skies,
   There's life in the old land yet!

THE CONFEDERATE FLAG.

BY J. R. BARRICK.

FLAG of the South! Flag of the free!
  Thy stars shall cheer each eye,
Thy folds a sacred banner be,
  To all beneath our sky;
From where the blue Ohio flows,
  Far to the sea-gulf's stream,
Borne by each gentle breath that blows,
  Thy hues shall flush and gleam.

Flag of the South! Flag of the free!
  Type of a new estate,
Thy folds shall wave o'er land and sea,
  And heart and home elate;
At thy approach shall tyrants quail
  And despots, trembling, flee;
Nor wrong thy sway of right assail —
  Nought mar thy liberty.

Flag of the South! Flag of the free!
  Bright symbol of a land
Wrung from the grasp of tyranny,
  Ere fettered heart and hand;

Freedom fixed in thy firm embrace,
  A home for age shall find,
Linking the high hopes of our race,
  With the grand march of mind.

Flag of the South ! Flag of the free !
  The one to which we clung
In years agone, hath ceased to be
  The pride on which we hung ;
Long trampled in the dust, that flag
  Hath lost the charm it bore ;
No longer vale, and glen, and crag,
  Swell with its praise of yore.

Flag of the South ! Flag of the free !
  Type of the Land of Flowers ;
Thy stars shall light our victory
  O'er all contending powers ;
Where law and order still shall reign,
  Thou shalt a signal be
To man, that he may still attain
  The boon of Liberty !

    GLASGOW, KY.

"STONEWALL JACKSON'S WAY."

COME, stack arms, men! Pile on the rails,
  Stir up the camp-fire bright;
No matter if the canteen fails,
  We 'll make a roaring night.
Here Shenandoah brawls along,
There burly Blue Ridge echoes strong,
To swell the brigade's rousing song
  Of " Stonewall Jackson's Way."

We see him now — the old slouched hat
  Cocked o'er his eye askew,
The shrewd, dry smile, the speech so pat,
  So calm, so blunt, so true.
The " Blue-Light Elder " knows 'em well;
Says he, " That's Banks — he 's fond of shell ;
Lord save his soul! we 'll give him —— " well,
  That 's "Stonewall Jackson's way."

Silence! ground arms! kneel all! caps off!
  Old Blue-Light 's going to pray.
Strangle the fool that dares to scoff!
  Attention! it 's his way.
Appealing from his native sod,
In *forma pauperis* to God —
" Lay bare thine arm, stretch forth thy rod !
  Amen !"   That 's " Stonewall's way."

He's in the saddle now. Fall in!
  Steady! the whole brigade!
Hill's at the ford, cut off — we'll win
  His way out, ball and blade!
What matter if our shoes are worn?
What matter if our feet are torn?
" Quick-step! we're with him before dawn!"
  That's " Stonewall Jackson's way."

The sun's bright lances rout the mists
  Of morning, and by George!
Here's Longstreet struggling in the lists,
  Hemmed in an ugly gorge.
Pope and his Yankees, whipped before,
" Bay'nets and grape!" near Stonewall roar;
" Charge, Stuart! Pay off Ashby's score!"
  Is " Stonewall Jackson's way."

Ah! maiden, wait and watch and yearn
  For news of Stonewall's band!
Ah! widow, read with eyes that burn
  That ring upon thy hand.
Ah! wife, sew on, pray on, hope on!
Thy life shall not be all forlorn.
The foe had better ne'er been born
  That gets in " Stonewall's way. "

BURN THE COTTON.

BY ESTELLE.

BURN the cotton! burn the cotton!
  Let the solemn triumph rise;
Fanned by Freedom's breath, its white wing
  Spreads her banner to the skies.
"Melt the bells" is but reëchoed
  O'er our valley's gathered pride,
Lay the cotton on the altar
  Where our loved have nobly died.

Burn the cotton! burn the cotton!
  Does this sacrifice compare
With the battle-field red flowing
  With the brave hearts offered there?
They no more shall strike for Freedom,
  Never worship at her shrine—
To hurl back the fell invader,
  To avenge them—it is thine.

Burn the cotton! burn the cotton!
  Down the Mississippi's tide
Let it thunder, till its valleys
  Catch the echo, far and wide—

Frowning in its wrath, it rises,
  Spreads its dark wing o'er the land,
Vetoes in its swelling fury,
  Gain, to lure the robber band.

Burn the cotton! burn the cotton!
  Pile the white fleece high and higher,
Till the heavens reflect the glory
  Kindled by the patriot's fire.
This shall teach the haughty foeman,
  Startle him too late, to find
Chains were never made for freemen,
  Chains the Southern heart to bind.

Burn the cotton! burn the cotton!
  Flaming sparks, instead of seed,
Shall be sown in death and terror
  To the mongrel Yankee breed;
And the *crowns* who nod attendance
  On the treacherous Federal's lure,
Feel too late the want and ruin,
  Unjust favor cannot cure.

Burn the cotton! burn the cotton!
  Let the record boldly stand;
Not a bale for " filthy lucre " —
  All for Freedom to our land.

Burn the cotton ! burn the cotton !
　　From its ashes there shall spring
Heralds of a new-born nation,
　　Claiming still that " Cotton 's King ! "

Memphis, Tenn., *May* 16, 1862.

———◆———

THE PRINTERS OF VIRGINIA TO "OLD ABE."

BY HARRY C. TREAKLE.

THOUGH we 're exempt, we 're not the *metal*
　　To keep in when duty calls ;
But onward we will *press*, to settle
　　This knotty *case*, with leaden *balls ;*
For our dear old mother State, the *fount*
　　From which we each our life did *take,*
Is *locked up* by a Vandal horde,
　　And the honor of the *craft* 's at stake.

For *lean-faced* Lincoln 's after us —
　　His slim *shanks* moving like a scout ;
But long before his *job* is done,
　　He 'll find that all his *quads* are out.
For with Lee our *headline* — worthy *guide* —
　　We, *galley*-slaves will never be,
But still *press* onward by his side,
　　For that *fat take*, sweet liberty !

Soon Abe will find, what he 's about
  Will cost him such a pile of rocks,
Before his cherished *work* is *out*,
  He 'll have no *sorts* in any *box !*
For his *bank* is now so very low,
  He scarce can *chase* up *quoins* to pay
The hired scum, the foreign foe,
  Who comes to steal our rights away.

And his *chums* now see, by his *foul matter*,
  To set *clean proof* he ne'er was *cast*,
And fears are felt that the gaunt old *ratter*
  Will go *broadside* to *hell* at last,
Where his friend, the *devil*, will welcome him,
  With *accents* sweet — to his bosom fly,
Revise his *foul proof-sheets* once more,
  And *knock* his naked *form* in *pi*.

And so, to rush the base old *monk* along,
  And bring the quiet soon about,
We 'll swell our *lines* to *columns* strong,
  And give no quarters till he 's *out ;*
For Southern *jours.* now take a *stand*,
  Their *foreman* marshalled at their *head*,
And each with *shooting-stick* in hand,
  Resolved they will his *matter lead*.

And while a foe is in the field,
  Our *hands* still steady, our *leaders* cool,
Death we 'll *em-brace* before we 'll yield;
  But, by God's help, we 'll *stick* and *rule*,
And when in after years to come,
  Our history 's read by youth and sage,
They 'll make a *side note* of " well done,"
  On this our *volume's* brightest *page*.

·Norfolk, Va., *April* 4, 1862.

———◆———

THE MARSEILLES HYMN.

TRANSLATED AND ADAPTED AS AN ODE,

BY E. F. PORTER, OF ALABAMA.

SONS of the South, arise! awake! be free!
  Behold! the day of Southern glory comes.
See where the blood-stained flag of tyranny
  Pollutes the air that breathes around your homes.
Rise! Southern men, from villages and farms,
  Cry vengeance! Oh! shall worse than pirate slaves
Strangle your children in their mothers' arms,
  And spit on dust that fills your fathers' graves?

To arms! sons of the South! Come like a moun-
          tain-flood;
March on! let every vale o'erflow with the in-
          vaders' blood.

What would these men, whose lives black treach-
          ery stains —
     Conspirators, to plunder long endeared?
For whom these vile, these ignominious chains —
     These fetters, for our brother's hands prepared?
Sons of the South, for us! Oh! bitter thought!
     What transports should our burning souls inspire!
Shall Southern men, by mercenaries bought,
     Be sold to vassalage, from son to sire?
To arms! sons of the South! Come like a moun-
          tain-flood;
March on! let every vale o'erflow with the in-
          vaders' blood.

What! shall this grovelling race, who cringe for gold,
     Make laws for Southern men, on Southern soil?
Shall these degenerate hordes, to avarice sold,
     Crush Freedom's sons, and Freedom's altars spoil?
Great God! oh! by these iron-shackled hands,
     Ne'er shall our necks beneath their yokes be led.
Of despots such as these, shall Southern bands
     Ne'er own the mastery, till every heart is dead.

To arms! sons of the South! Come like a moun-
    tain-flood;
March on! let every vale o'erflow with the in-
    vaders' blood.

Tremble, O tyrants! and you, perfidious tools,
  Of every race and party long the scorn!
Tremble, ye base, ye parricidal fools,
  The doom of treachery is already born.
All Southern men are heroes in the fray;
  If fall they must, o'erpowered in the field,
Long as the race endures, each child for aye
  Shall from his cradle strike the sounding shield.
To arms! sons of the South! Come like a moun-
    tain flood;
March on! let every vale o'erflow with the in-
    vaders' blood.

Sons of the South! magnanimous in war,
  Strike or withhold, as honor bids, your blows.
Spare, if you will, those victims from afar,
  Who, ignorant of liberty, become your foes.
But for these bastards of a free-born bed,
  These parasites, in Freedom's arms caressed,
These beasts, by sin and spoil and rapine bred,
  Who dig for blood, deep in their mother's breast,

To arms ! sons of the South !   Come like a moun-
    tain-flood ;
March on ! let every vale o'erflow with the in-
    vaders' blood.

O sacred love of country !   For the South,
  Come, brave avengers, rush to every field.
Let cries of " Liberty " from every mouth
  Sound the alarm, till the base traitors yield.
Under our glorious flag, let Victory
  Respond to Freedom's call.   Wipe off the stain
Of the invaders' feet.   Dying, they will see
  Thy triumph, and the land redeemed again.
To arms ! sons of the South !   Come like a moun-
    tain flood ;
March on ! let every vale o'erflow with the in-
    vaders' blood.

                          Nashville Gazette.

THE TIMES.

BY KATE.

Inscribed to all " God's Freemen."

COME, list to my song,
  It will not be long,
Of a war-fire cursing our Nation ;
  By demagogues cruel,

With *Republican fuel* —
It threatens our land's desolation.

" Old Abe " was elected,
Just what I expected,
" *Chief ruler*," " *Chief Justice*," " *the law;* "
But, since they 've crown'd him,
Wise men have found him
A Northern fanatic's gewgaw.

On a " platform " he stands
Of " *free niggers*," " *free lands*,"
" *Free all*," save a freeman's communion ;
A " *splitter* " his trade,
Thus a " *wedge* " he has made,
Of war, to dissever the Union.

He is spoken of freely
Through *Monitor Greely*,
Who stands at the head of the " stairs,"
On the " *planks of Chicago*,"
As bold as " Iago, "
And curses all Southern affairs.

The South this have taken,
And cannot be shaken,

It matters not what they assert ;
    They 'll " poke at 'em fun,
    Like that of " *Bull Run*,"
And say, with *Abe*, " *nobody 's hurt !* "

    I 've heard it before,
    Down in Baltimore,
Of " *mixing with water strychnine* " —
    ' T was said that old Butler,
    (Abraham's sutler)
Was this " Borgia," or vile " Cataline."

    At no distant day,
    All freemen will say,
Thus rightly give *A be* his desert ;
    " This war we ignore —
    We've told you before,
It must cease, or ' somebody 's hurt.' "

    Then England with France,
    And Spain, too, may dance,
We 'll ask not, nor care not about them ;
    For with all united,
    (If the South is arighted)
We 'll laugh and live happy without them.

    Fairfax Court House, Va.

THINKING OF THE SOLDIERS.

WE were sitting around the table,
  Just a night or two ago,
In the little cosy parlor,
  With the lamp-light burning low,
And the window-blinds half opened,
  For the summer air to come,
And the painted curtains moving
  Like a busy pendulum.

O! the cushions on the sofa,
  And the pictures on the wall,
And the gathering of comforts,
  In the old familiar hall;
And the wagging of the pointer,
  Lounging idly by the door,
And the flitting of the shadows
  From the ceiling to the floor.

O! they wakened in my spirit,
  Like the beautiful in art,
Such a busy, busy thinking —
  Such a dreaminess of heart,
That I sat among the shadows,
  With my spirit all astray;

Thinking only — thinking only
  Of the soldiers far away ;

Of the tents beneath the moonlight,
  Of the stirring tattoo's sound,
Of the soldier in his blanket,
  In his blanket on the ground ;
Of the icy winter coming,
  Of the cold bleak winds that blow,
And the soldier in his blanket,
  In his blanket on the snow.

Of the blight upon the heather,
  And the frost upon the hill,
And the whistling, whistling ever,
  And the never, never still ;
Of the little leaflets falling,
  With the sweetest, saddest sound —
And the soldier — oh ! the soldier,
  In his blanket on the ground.

Thus I lingered in my dreaming,
  In my dreaming far away,
Till the spirit's picture-painting
  Seemed as vivid as the day ;
And the moonlight faded softly
  From the window opened wide,

And the faithful, faithful pointer
  Nestled closer by my side.

And I knew that 'neath the starlight,
  Though the chilly frosts may fall,
That the soldier will be dreaming,
  Dreaming often of us all.
So I gave my spirit's painting
  Just the breathing of a sound,
For the dreaming, dreaming soldier,
  In his slumber on the ground.

November 24, 1861.

A SOUTHERN SCENE.

O MAMMY! have you heard the news?"
  Thus spake a Southern child,
As in the nurse's aged face
  She upward glanced and smiled.

" What news you mean, my little one?
  It must be mighty fine
To make my darling's face so red,
  Her sunny blue eyes shine."

" Why Abram Lincoln, don't you know,
    The Yankee President,
Whose ugly picture once we saw,
    When up to town we went, —

" Well, he is going to free you all,
    And make you rich and grand,
And you 'll be dressed in silk and gold,
    Like the proudest in the land.

" A gilded coach shall carry you
    Where'er you wish to ride ;
And, mammy, all your work shall be
    Forever laid aside."

The eager speaker paused for breath,
    And then the old nurse said,
While closer to her swarthy cheek
    She pressed the golden head : —

" My little missus, stop and res' —
    You' talking mighty fas' ;
Jes' look up dere, and tell me what
    You see in yonder glass ?

" You sees old mammy's wrinkly face,
    As black as any coal ;

And underneath her handkerchief
   Whole heaps of knotty wool.

" My darlin's face is red and white,
   Her skin is soff and fine,
And on her pretty little head
   De yallar ringlets shine.

" My chile, who made dis difference
   'Twixt mammy and 'twixt you ?
You reads de dear Lord's blessed book,
   And you can tell me true.

" De dear Lord said it must be so;
   And, honey, I for one,
Wid tankful heart will always say,
   His holy will be done.

" I tanks mas' Linkum all de same,
   But when I wants for free,
I 'll ask de Lord of glory,
   Not poor buckra man like he.

" And as for gilded carriages,
   Dey 's notin' 't all to see ;
My massa's coach, what carries him,
   Is good enough for me.

" And, honey, when your mammy wants
  To change her homespun dress,
She 'll pray like dear old missus,
  To be clothed with righteousness.

" My work 's been done dis many a day,
  And now I takes my ease,
A waitin' for de Master's call,
  Jes' when de Master please.

" And when at las' de time 's done come,
  And poor old mammy dies,
Your own dear mother's soff white hand
  Shall close dese tired old eyes.

" De dear Lord Jesus soon will call
  Old mammy home to him,
And He can wash my guilty soul
  From ebery spot of sin.

" And at His feet I shall lie down,
  Who died and rose for me ;
And den, and not till den, my chile,
  Your mammy will be free.

" Come, little missus, say your prayers ;
  Let old mas' Linkum 'lone,

The debil knows who b'longs to him,
And he 'll take care of his own."

PENSACOLA : TO MY SON.

BY M. S.

BEAUTIFUL the land may be,
  Its groves of palm, its laurel trees,
And o'er the smiling, murm'ring sea,
  Soft may blow the Southern breeze —
And land, and sea, and balmy air,
May make a home of beauty there.

And bright beneath Floridian sky,
  The world to thy young fancy seems;
I see the light that fills thine eye,
  I know what spirit rules thy dreams;
But flower-gemmed shore and rippling sea
Are darker than the grave to me;

For storms are lowering in that sky,
  And sad may be that fair land's doom;
Full soon, perhaps, the battle-cry
  May wake the cannon's fearful boom,

And shot and shell from o'er the waves
May plough the rose's bed for graves.

And we, whose dear ones cluster there, ·
    We, mothers, who have let them go —
Our all, perhaps — how shall we bear
    That which another week may show ?
The love which made our lives, all gone,
Our hearts left desolate and lone !

Country ! what to *me* that name,
    Should I in vain demand my son ?
Glory ! what a nation's fame ?
    Home ! home, without thee, I have none ;
Ah ! stay — this Southern land not *mine ?*
The land that e'en in death is thine !

A country's laurel-wreath for thee,
    A hero's grave — my own ! my own !
And neither land nor home for *me*,
    Because a *mother's* hope is gone ?
Traitor I am !   God's laws command
That, NEXT TO HEAVEN, OUR NATIVE LAND !

And I will not retract — ah ! no —
    What, in my pride of home, I said,
That, " *I would give my son to go*

Where'er our HERO RULER *led!"*
The mother's heart may burst — but still,
Make it, O God, to know Thy will.

NEW ORLEANS, La.

———◆———

THE WAR-STORM.

BY C. J. H.

OFTEN by a treacherous sea-side
    I have heard the ocean's roar,
Often, at its ebb or flood tide,
    Listened to its mystic lore.

Sometimes it would whisper to me
    Words of smooth and liquid tone,
And its pictures, memory drew me,
    Sweet as breath from tropic zone;

Ever to me sang its story,
    Ever to me talked the sea;
Evening sun would paint its glory,
    Bringing sober thoughts to me.

I would think how like the passions
    Is the smooth or stormy sea;

Breath of heat or cold may fashion
  Rage, or hope, or gloom, or glee.

I, to-day, have seen the flood-tide
  Of our country's strength and youth,
Plain as waves upon the sea-side,
  And as mighty as is truth.

No faint breath has caused this motion,
  No faint ripple raised this storm;
But like tempest o'er the ocean —
  In the summer, calm and warm —

We have listened to the muttering
  Of the thunder in the sky,
Till at length its mighty uttering
  Is the battle's wildest cry.

Stormy clouds, of blackest error,
  Drove along this battle-car,
Freighted it with bloody terror,
  And plunged us in this fearful war.

Rain of lead we know will rattle,
  Steel will flash, and blood will flow,
Cannon thunder through the battle,
  And its ending none can know.

Yes ! there is a glorious lightness
  In the soldier's scarlet shroud ;
History touches it with brightness ;
  Fame will sound his requiem loud ;

Lasting as the long forever,
  Reaching ages as they come,
Telling round the fireside, ever,
  How he died defending home.

———◆———

THE VOLUNTEERS TO THE "MELISH."

BY WM. C. ESTRES.

COME forth, ye gallant heroes,
  Rub up each rusty gun,
And face these hireling Yankees,
  Who live by tap of drum.
We Volunteers are wearied,
  By a twelve months' " sojourn ; "
We want to rest a little,
  And then we 'll fight " again."

We 've won some five pitched battles,
  But will yield you our " polish ; "

And if you want some glory,
   Why pitch in now, " Melish."
Don't refuse to leave your spouses ;
   Our own are just as dear,
And each lonely little woman
   Longs for her Volunteer.

Don't mind your sobbing sweethearts ;
   For though 't is hard to part,
We 'll volunteer to chase 'em,
   And console each troubled heart.
For the sake of old Virginia,
   Come and fight ! *that 's if you can,*
And let your prattling babies
   Know their daddy was a man.

For you *we 've* fought and struggled ;
   Had " no furloughs " — nary one —
We want a little resting,
   And so we 're coming home.
Then *forward*, bold Militia !
   " If you 're coming, come along,"
Or, by the gods ! we 'll force you out
   To your duty — right or wrong.

THE GIRLS OF THE MONUMENTAL CITY.

WRITTEN BY A CONFEDERATE PRISONER.

DAUGHTERS of the sunny South,
  Where Freedom loves to dwell,
How rare your charms, how sweet your smiles,
  No mortal lips can tell;
Your native hills, the rippling rills,
  The echo wild and free,
Declare you born to hate and scorn
  All Northern tyranny.

Girls whose smiles are all reserved,
  The Southern youth to bless;
Whose hearts are kept for those who fight
  For Freedom's happiness;
Your spirits bold, so now unfold
  What willingly you would do,
Where Yankee spirit — the tyrants might
  Not wield against you.

For you your loving brothers rush
  To overthrow the invader's might —
On martial field the sword they wield,
  And Yankee cowards smite.

14

May heaven bless, with bright success,
    Each glorious Southern son;
Be this your prayer, O maidens fair!
    And our freedom will be won.

Southern girls, on this we 've sworn,
    The South *must — shall be free —*
No Northern shackles will be worn;
    To them we 'll bend no knee.
From hill to hill, exultant, shrill,
    Our battle-cry rings forth:
Freedom or death on every breath,
    And hatred to the North.

Cease not to smile, brave Southern girls,
    On our efforts to be free —
Whilst life remains, we 'll struggle on,
    Till all the world shall see
That those who fight for home and right
    Can never be enslaved;
Their blood may stain the battle-plain;
    Our country must be saved.

BALTIMORE, Md., *March*, 1862.

GONE TO THE BATTLE-FIELD.

BY JOHN ANTROBUS.

THE reaper has left the field,
  The mower has left the plain ;
And the reaper's hook, and the mower's scythe,
  Are changed to the sword again ;
For the voice of a hundred years ago,
When Freedom struck her mightiest blow,
  Thrills every heart and brain.

The way-side mill is still,
  And the wheel drips all alone,
For the miller's brother, and son, and sire,
  And the miller's self have gone ;
And their wives and daughters, tarrying still,
With smiles and tears about the mill,
  Wave, wave their heroes on.

The grain is full and ripe,
  And the harvest-moon is nigh,
But the farmer's son is among the slain,
  And the father heard the cry ;
And his ancient eyes flashed fires of old,
His hoary head rose strong and bold,
  As wild, he hurried by.

The corn is yet a-field,
  But many a stalk is red;
Yet not with the autumn-tassel stained,
  But the blood of heroes shed;
And their blood cries out from heaven, of slain:
Oh, brothers, leave the sheaves of grain;
  On, to the fields of the dead!

But every quiet farm,
  Whence father and son had gone,
The fairest daughters of the land,
  Brave-hearted, cheer us on,
With the tender smiles that shelter tears,
And words to thrill a soldier's ears,
  When bloody fields are won.

Scarcely the form of man
  Was seen on the long highway;
But patriot age, whose withered hands
  Stretched feebly up to pray,
And children whose voices haunt us still,
Gathered on every knoll and hill,
  Cheering us on our way.

Yonder, with feeble limbs,
  A matron, with silver hair,
Knelt, trembling, down on the soldier's path,

And breathed to heaven a prayer ;
With quivering lips, with streaming eyes,
O God ! preserve these gallant boys.
  In battle, be Thou there.

O, soldiers ! such as these
  Like household memories come ;
For a thousand prayers ascend to-day
  From those we left at home ;
For the red, red field, to-night may be
Our couch, our grave, while Victory
  Shall shout above our tomb.

In battle's bloody hour
  These pictures shall arise,
Of mothers, sisters, wives, and homes,
  And red and streaming eyes ;
And every arm shall stronger be,
For home, for God, for liberty,
  And strike, while mercy dies.

HEAD-QUARTERS, *9th Regt. Virginia Vols.*

----♦----

THE DEBT.

REMEMBER, men of Maryland,
  You have a debt to pay,
A debt which years of patience
  Will never wear away ;

Which must be paid at last, although
  Our dearest blood it cost;
A debt which *shall* be paid, unto
  The very uttermost.

We owe for confidence betrayed
  By those we trusted best;
The sword we gave them to unsheathe,
  They turned against our breast;
For spies, that noted down our words,
  The while they shared our bread;
For hounds that even dared disturb
  The quiet of the dead.

We owe for all the love they lied,
  The wolfish hate they showed;
For all those glittering bayonets
  That meet us on the road;
For black suspicion, deadlier far
  Than flash of Northern swords;
For treason threatened at our hearths,
  And poison at our boards.

For many a deed of darkness done
  Beneath their " Stripes and Stars;"
For women outraged in their homes,
  And fired on in the cars;

For those black tiers of cannon trained
  To bear on Baltimore ;
We owe for friends in prison kept,
  And Davis in his gore.

Wrongs such as these — aye, more than these —
  Make up our fearful debt,
And many a gallant heart has sworn,
  It shall be settled yet.
Each moment near and nearer brings
  That solemn reckoning day ;
And when it comes — and when it comes,
  Remember — and repay !

BEYOND THE POTOMAC.

BY PAUL H. HAYNE.*

THEY slept on the fields which their valor had
    won !
But arose with the first early blush of the sun,
For they knew that a great deed remained to be
    done,
    When they passed o'er the River.

---

* This piece was originally published in the *Richmond
Whig* at the time of "Stonewall" Jackson's last raid into
Maryland, and we believe was not copied by any of the
Northern papers.—*The Round Table.*

They rose with the sun, and caught life from his
    light —
Those giants of courage, those Anaks in fight —
And they laughed out aloud in the joy of their
    might,
      Marching swift for the River.

On! on! like the rushing of storms through the
    hills —
On! on! with a tramp that is firm as their wills —
And the one heart of thousands grows buoyant and
    thrills,
      At the thought of the River.

On! the sheen of their swords! the fierce gleam of
    their eyes
It seemed as on earth a new sunlight would rise,
And king-like, flash up to the sun in the skies,
      O'er the path to the River.

But their banners, shot-scarred, and all darkened
    with gore,
On a strong wind of morning streamed wildly
    before,
Like the wings of Death-angels swept fast to the
    shore,
      The green shore of the River.

As they march — from the hill-side, the hamlet, the
    stream —
Gaunt throngs whom the Foeman had manacled,
    teem,
Like men just roused from some terrible dream,
      To pass o'er the River.

They behold the broad banners, blood-darkened,
    yet fair,
And a moment dissolves the last spell of despair,
While a peal as of victory swells on the air,
      Rolling out to the River.

And that cry, with a thousand strange echoings
    spread,
Till the ashes of heroes seemed stirred in their
    bed,
And the deep voice of passion surged up from the
    dead —
      Aye! press on to the River.

On! on! like the rushing of storms through the
    hills,
On! on! with a tramp that is firm as their wills,
And the one heart of thousands grows buoyant,
    and thrills,
      As they pause by the River.

Then the wan face of Maryland, haggard, and worn,
At that sight, lost the touch of its aspect forlorn,
And she turned on the Foeman full statured in
      scorn,
    Pointing stern to the River.

And Potomac flowed calm, scarcely heaving her
      breast,
With her low-lying billows all bright in the west,
For the hand of the Lord lulled the waters to rest
    Of the fair rolling River.

Passed! passed! the glad thousands march safe
      through the tide.
(Hark, Despot! and hear the wild knell of your
      pride,
Ringing weird-like and wild, pealing up from the
      side
    Of the calm flowing River.)

'Neath a blow swift and mighty the Tyrant shall
      fall,
Vain! vain! to his God swells a desolate call,
For his grave has been hollowed, and woven his
      pall,
    Since they passed o'er the River.

THE CONFEDERATE FLAG.

BRIGHT banner of freedom, with pride I unfold
    thee;
Fair flag of my country, with love I behold thee,
Gleaming above us, in freshness and youth,
Emblem of liberty — symbol of truth;
For this flag of my country in triumph shall wave
O'er the Southerner's home and the Southerner's
    grave.

All bright are the stars that are beaming upon us,
And bold are the bars that are gleaming above us;
The one shall increase in their number and light,
The other grow bolder in power and might;
For this flag of my country in triumph shall wave
O'er the Southerner's home or the Southerner's
    grave.

Those bars of bright red show our firm resolution
To die, if need be, shielding thee from pollution;
For man in this hour must give all he holds dear,
And woman her prayers and her words of high
    cheer,
If they wish this fair banner in triumph to wave
O'er the Southerner's home and the Southerner's
    grave.

To the great God of battle we look with reliance;
On our fierce Northern foe with contempt and de-
    fiance;
For the South shall smile on in her fragrance and
    bloom
When the North is fast sinking in silence and gloom;
For the flag of our country in triumph must wave
O'er the Southerner's home or the Southerner's
    grave.

THE SOUTH.

BY CHARLIE WILDWOOD.

THE bright rose of beauty, unnurtured by art,
    And purity's lily doth thrive in thy heart,
While honor hath crowned thee with glory's bright
    ray,
And Flora hath deck'd thee with flowers of May.
Oh, beautiful South! cherished home of my birth,
Thou fairest, thou loveliest land of the earth!
My heart, like the ivy, still clings unto thee,
Oh, beautiful, beautiful land of the free!
    Chorus — The South! the South! my own beau-
        tiful South!
        Land of chivalry! home of liberty!

> Fondly I love thee, dear land of the
> South!
> Dear land of the South! dear land of
> the South!

Dear liberty, virtue, and truth, most sublime,
The flowers that bloom in that sun-smiling clime,
And these the base tyrant would crush to the
earth,
And mangle and bruise on the soil of their birth.
All crimson thy land, with the life-glowing flood,
And dabble his hands in thy heart's reeking blood !
But oh ! by the God of the righteous and free,
Bright region ! it never ! no, never ! shall be.

Like swarms of foul demons, his minions come
down,
And their war-rusted weapons insultingly frown,
To fright thy fair fields with their bloody alarms,
And rob thee, dear land, of all of thy charms.
But thy free spirit still rides on the swift gale,
Like the eagle that sweeps o'er the mountain and
dale ;
And thy sons, they rush forth with the courage of
men,
To fight, and to bleed, and to conquer again.

The tyrant, with shackles, would manacle thee,—
Would strangle thy spirit, dear land of the free,
Would trample the banner of right in the dust,
And yoke thee with iron, proud queen of the
    just !
But the hearts of thy sons, unappalled by a fear,
As their swords leap up fiercely and flame in the
    air,
Now swear that it never ! no ! never ! shall be,
Bright queen of the lovely ! sweet home of the
    free !

——◆——

SONG.

R EBEL is a sacred name ;
    Traitor, too, is glorious ;
By such names our fathers fought —
    By them were victorious.
Chorus — Gaily floats our rebel flag
        Over hill and valley —
        Broad its bars, and bright its stars,
        Calling us to rally.

Washington a rebel was,
    Jefferson a traitor,—
But their treason won success,
    And made their glory greater.

O 'er our Southern sunny strand
    Vandal feet are treading,
And the Hessians on our land
    Devastation spreading.

Can you, then, inactive be ?
    Maidens fair are saying ;
And their bright eyes shame us out
    With this long delaying.

Rouse ye, children of the free,
    Rally to our streamer ;
The vandal flag floats on our land, —
    Awaken, Southern dreamer !

Rebel arms shall win the fight,
    Rebel prayers defend us,
Rebel maidens greet us home,
    When tyrants no more rend us.

This song was written by an inmate of the Old-Capitol Prison in Washington city, and sung by his fellow-prisoners. — *Richmond Sentinel.*

BATTLE-SONG OF THE INVADED.

THE foe! the foe! They come! they come!
  Light up the beacon pyre;
Let every hill and mountain home
  Give back the signal fire,
And wave the red cross on the night,
  The blood-red cross of war, —
What though we perish in the fight!
  Our fathers died before!

Up, meet the foe, on to the strife;
  For freemen's blades we hold,
And hands that fight for land and life
  Fight not those for gold.
Give shout and banners to the gale,
  The trumpet, peal it forth,
Till our sons beàr down from every vale
  Like snow-flakes from the North.

Hark! lo their shouts upon the breeze,
  Their banners in the sun,
And like the thunder of the seas
  Their deep tread thunders on.
We 'll meet them here on each bold height,
  In every glen make head —

And give the battle to the right ; —
  We will be free or dead.

We stand on sacred, holy ground,
  Where thousand memories meet ;
Our father's homes are all around,
  Their graves beneath our feet ;
Our roofs are mouldering far and wide,
  That late smiled in the sun ;
Our brides are weeping at our sides ;
  Gods ! let them come on !

Hurrah ! hurrah ! he gleams in sight ;
  It fires the brain to see
How the proud spoiler flashes bright
  In war's gay panoply.
We 'll show him that our fathers' brands
  Nor rust nor time can stay ;
With tramp and shouts, bold hearts and hands,
  Up, freemen, and away !

The work is done, the strife is o'er,
  The whirlwinds thundered by, —
There 's not from hill to ocean shore
  A foeman left to die.
Our brides are thronging every height,
  They wave us weeping home ;

God gives the battle to the right, —
Back to our hearth-stones come.

THE TURTLE.

CÆSAR, afloat with his fortunes !
  And all the world agog,
Straining its eyes
At a thing that lies
  In the water, like a log !
It 's a weasel ! a whale !
I see its tail !
  It 's a porpoise ! a polywog !

Tarnation ! it 's a *turtle !*
  And blast my bones and skin,
My hearties, sink her,
Or else you 'll think her
  A regular terror — pin !

The frigate poured a broadside !
  The bombs they whistled well,
But — hit old Nick
With a sugar stick !
  It didn't phase her shell !

Piff, from the creature's larboard —
  And dipping along the water
A bullet hissed
From a wreath of mist
  Into a Doodle's quarter !

Raff, from the creature's starboard —
  Rip, from his ugly snorter,
And the Congress and
The Cumberland
  Sunk, and nothing — shorter.

Now, here's to you, Virginia,
  And you are bound to win !
By your rate of bobbing round
  And your way of pitchin' in —
For you are a cross
Of the old sea-horse
  And a regular terror — pin.

SOUTHERN BATTLE-SONG.

AIR — " *Bruce's Address.* "

RAISE the Southern flag on high !
  Shout aloud the battle-cry !

Let its echoes reach the sky —
   "God and Southern Rights!"

Sons of wealth, and sons of toil,
Will ye yield your lands for spoil,
Drive the foe from Southern soil!
   Glory now invites.

Rally round our banners bright,
Let its stars of quenchless light
Dim the base invader's sight,
   On the battle-field.

When the death-clouds darkly lower,
When the cannons blaze and roar,
Though its folds be drenched in gore,
   We will never yield.

Lo! upon our sacred land,
Lincoln's arméd hirelings stand;
Haste to crush the dastard band!
   Win a patriot's name.

On the fields of battle grow
Laurels for the soldier's brow
Forward, boys, and gather now,
   Wreaths of endless fame.

By our sires who. fought and bled !
By Virginia's honored dead !
By the blood so lately shed !
We will *make* them know,

Southern hearts are true as steel,
Wrongs like ours are *slow* to heal,
Sooner will we *die* than kneel
. To a Northern foe.

JACKSON.

BY HARRY FLASH.

NOT midst the lightning of the stormy fight,
Not in the rush upon the vandal foe,
Did kingly Death, with his resistless might,
Lay the Great Leader low.

His warrior soul its earthly shackles broke
In the full sunshine of a peaceful town;
When all the storm was hushed, the trusty oak
That propped our cause, went down.

Though his alone the blood that flecks the ground,
Recording all his grand, heroic deeds,
Freedom herself is writhing with the wound,
And all the. country bleeds.

He entered not the Nation's Promised Land
At the red belching of the cannon's mouth;
But broke the House of Bondage with his hand—
    The Moses of the South!

O gracious God! not gainless is the loss:
A glorious sunbeam gilds thy sternest frown;
And while his country staggers with the cross,
    He rises with the crown!

———◆———

SONG OF THE PRIVATEER.

BY ALEX. H. CUMMINS.

FEARLESSLY the seas we roam,
    Tossed by each briny wave;
Its boundless surface is our home,
    Its bosom deep our grave.
No foreign mandate fills with awe
    Our gallant-hearted band;
We know no home, we know no law,
    But that of Dixie's land.

The bright star is our compass true,
    Our chart the ocean wide;

Our only hope the noble few
  That 's standing side by side.
We do not fear the stormy gale
  That sweeps old ocean's strand;
We scorn our enemy's clumsy sail,
  And all for Dixie's land.

We love to hoist to the topmost peak
  Our Southern Stars and Stripes;
And woe to him who dares to seek
  To trample on their rights!
It is the ægis of the free,
  And by it we will stand,
And watch it waving o'er the sea,
  And over Dixie's land.

We love to roam the deep, deep sea,
  And hear the cannon's boom,
And give the war-cry wild and free
  Amid the battle's gloom.
We do not fight alone for gain,
  So far from native strand;
But our country's freedom and its fame,
  And the fair of Dixie's land.

NO UNION MEN.

BY MILLIE MAYFIELD.

"On the 21st, five of the enemy's steamers approached Washington, N. C., and landed a hundred Yankees, who marched through the town, playing 'Yankee Doodle,' hoisted their flag on the Court House, and destroyed gun-carriages and an unfinished gunboat in the ship-yard. The people preserved a sullen and unresisting silence. The Yankees then left, saying they were disappointed in not finding Union men." — *Telegram from Charleston, March 29th, 1862.*

UNION MEN!" O thrice-fooled fools!
   As well might ye hope to bind
The desert sands with a silken thread,
   When tossed by the whirling wind,
Or to blend the shattered waves that lash
   The feet of the cleaving rock,
When the tempest walks the face of the deep,
   And the water-spirits mock,
As the severed chain to reunite
   In a peaceful link again;
On our burning homesteads ye may write,
   "We found no Union men."

Aye, hoist your old dishonored flag,
   And pipe your worn-out tune;
The hills of the South have caught the strain,
   And will answer it full soon;
Not with the sycophantic tone,
   And the cringing knee bent low —
The deep-mouthed cannon shall bear the tale,
   Where the sword deals blow for blow;
Our braying trumpets in your ears,
   Shall defiant shout again,
" Back, wolves and foxes, to your lairs,
   Here are no Union men!"

Union, with tastes dissimilar?
   Such union is the worst
And direst form of bondage that
   Nations or men have cursed!
Union with traitors? Hear ye not
   That cry for vengeance, deep,
Where hand to hand, and foot to foot,
   Our glittering columns sweep?
Our iron-tongued artillery
   Shouts through the bristling glen,
To the war-drum echoing reviellé,
   " Here are no Union men!"

Oh, deep have sunken the burning seeds
   That the winged winds have borne,

That for all your future years must yield
    The thistle and prison-thorn ;
Our soil was genial — ye might have sown
    A harvest rich, 't is too late !
To our children's children we leave for you
    But a heritage of Hate !
Ye have open'd the wild floodgates of war,
    And we may not the torrent pen ;
But ye seek in vain on our stormbeat shore
    For the myth called " Union Men."

HARP OF THE SOUTH.

A SONNET.

HARP of the South, awake ! A loftier strain
    Than ever yet thy tuneful strings has stirred,
Awaits thee now. The Eastern world has heard
The thunder of the battle 'cross the main, —
Has seen the young South burst the tyrant's chain,
And rise to being at a single word —
The watchword, Liberty — so long transferred
To the oppressor's mouth. Moons wax and wane,
And still the nations stand with listening ear,
And still o'er ocean floats the battle-cry.

Harp of the South, awake, and bid them hear
The name of Jackson; loud, and clear, and high,
Strike notes exultant, o'er the hero's bier,
Who, though he sleeps in dust, can never die.

CORA.

——◆——

WHAT THE SPIRITS OF THE FATHERS OF THE FIRST REVOLUTION SAY TO THEIR SONS NOW ENGAGED IN THE SECOND.

BY HENRY LOMAS.

WE are watching that land where Liberty
    woke, —
Like beams of the morning through darkness it
    broke, —
Then up from the mountain the bold eagle sprung,
And wide to the breeze his broad pinions flung.
    Rise! rise! ye sons of the South and be
      free!

The mighty have fallen, yet death cannot chill,
Those noble emotions the soul ever thrill;
The grave hath no confines the spirit to hold,
While back to its kindred it flies to unfold
    Truth! Truth! safeguard of the South and
      the free.

Shall Washington rest, while a wail of discord
Reminds him the North is forgetting the Lord?
Will hero and statesman, — the country's bright
    light, —
Look down without pity from yonder far height,
      On this Land of Hope, for the brave and
      the free?

That same noble spirit now watches above,
With thousands of others, to guide and guard you
    with love;
For here, true, earnest, and brave men are found,
With hearts uncorrupted, to their native land
    bound.
      Awake! awake! O ye sons of the South,
      and be free!

Down with the hireling that seeks now to rend
The homes which your ancestors fought to de-
    fend;
Rekindle the beacon ere the last spark is fled,
And light up the camp-fires round Liberty's bed!
      Ye sons of the sunny South, strike to be
      free!

Fear not the Northern despot, or his feeble frown,

Who seeks, through his minions, the South to put
    down;
Look to your God, from whence comes all power,
And seek His aid and protection in each darkened
    hour.
      Strike again and again, O ye sons of the
      free !

Carolina's sons to this platform have come —
Protection to Liberty, to fireside, and home —
Their watchword to-day, as their Fathers' of old,
Truth, Justice, and Freedom, before Northern gold.
      Ye are the sons of the Fathers who bled to
      be free !

Then loud ring the anvil, the hammer, and bell ;
The South her new anthem, say what does it
    tell ; —
Cotton, Grain, and Sugar, have proved threefold
    cord —
Columbia, the envied, the blest of the Lord !
      Sun of the sunny land, shine still o'er the
      free !

On heaven's fair arches, see graven the names
Of patriot and soldier, who drained life's pure
    veins ;

Then down with the Northern despot, let him hide
    his head,
Who by heartless oppression would sever one
    thread
      Of this Southern Confederacy, the hope of
      the free.

Once again at the altar, brothers, gather and kneel;
Our pledge, the South — one family, in woe or in
    weal;
One God and one Country, — in peace or in war;
The South, Free, United, and Truth the polestar
      Of this sunny land, which for ye must be
      free !

HEART-VICTORIES.

BY A SOLDIER'S WIFE.

THERE's not a stately hall,
    There's not a cottage fair,
That proudly stands on Southern soil,
    Or softly nestles there,
But in its peaceful walls,
    With wealth or comfort blest,
A stormy battle fierce hath raged
    In gentle woman's breast.

There Love, the true, the brave,
  The beautiful, the strong,
Wrestles with Duty, gaunt and stern,
  Wrestles and struggles long;
He falls — no more again
  His giant foe to meet;
Bleeding at every opening vein,
  Love falls at Duty's feet.

Oh ! daughter of the South !
  No victor's crown be thine;
Not thine, upon the tented field,
  In martial pomp to shine;
But, with unfaltering trust
  In Him who rules on high,
To deck thy loved ones for the fray,
  And send them forth to die.

With wildly throbbing heart —
  With faint and trembling breath —
The maiden speeds her lover on,
  To victory or death;
Forth from caressing arms,
  The mother sends her son,
And bids him nobly battle on,
  Till the last field is won.

While she, the tried, the true,
  The loving wife of years,
Chokes down the rising agony,
  Drives back the starting tears:
"I yield thee up," she cries,
  "In the country's cause to fight;
Strike for our own, our children's home,
  And God defend the right."

Oh! daughters of the South,
  When our fair land is free,
When peace her lovely mantle throws
  Softly o'er land and sea,
History shall tell, how thou
  Hast nobly borne thy part,
And won the proudest triumphs yet, —
  The victories of the heart.

—◆—

TRUE-HEART SOUTHRONS.

Air — "*Blue Bonnets over the Border.*"

FOR trumpet and drum, leave the soft voice of
    maiden:
For the tramp of armed men, leave the maze of
    the dance;

One kiss on the lips, with words of love laden —
  One look in dimm'd eyes — then the rifle and
    lance.
Chorus.   March, march, true-heart Southrons,
        Fall into ranks and march in good
          order, —
        Escambia shall many a day tell of the
          fierce affray,
        When we drove the base Northmen
          far over our border.

Do ye weep, ye fair flowers, our hearthstones that
  brighten?
For every tear shed shall fall ten foemen's lives;
Far in the cold North their hosts we will frighten,
  As we strike for our " Homes, our sweethearts,
    and wives."
    March, march, &c.

THE IRISH BATTALION.

WHEN Old Virginia took the field,
  And wanted men to rally on —
To be at once her sword and shield —
  She formed her First Battalion.

Although her sons were Volunteers,
  And brave as ever bore a brand,
The good old lady had her fears
  That they might prove but weak of hand.

She therefore wisely cast about
  For men of mettle and of mould,
With nerve of steel and muscle stout,
  Like those that lived in days of old.

She wanted men of pluck and might,
  Of fiery heart and horny hand,
To wield a pick as well as fight,
  Or build a breastwork out of sand.

Or should she march to meet the foe,
  That threatened on her western border,
She wanted willing men to go,
  When told to put her roads in order.

Or should the Volunteers retreat,
  With baggage that might make them tarry,
'T would blunt the edge of their defeat
  To bear a hand and help them carry.

Or should some die of fell disease,—
  The surgeons having failed to save,—

Sure men who work with so much ease,
  Would volunteer to dig a grave !

For these, and reasons quite as sound,
  When Old Virginia went to war,
She circumspectly viewed the ground
  And plumped the middle man from taw !

In other words, to change the figure,
  When she stood up and took her rifle,
And put her finger on the trigger,
  She meant to work, and not to trifle.

And standing thus, yet wanting then
  Some regulars to rally on,
She took three hundred Irishmen
  And formed her First Battalion.

And when the storm of battle sweeps,
  Where fiercest foemen sally on,
There, hard at work, or piled in heaps,
  She 'll find her bold Battalion.

MONODY ON THE DEATH OF GENERAL STONEWALL JACKSON.

BY THE EXILE.

AYE, toll! toll! toll!
　　Toll the funeral bell!
And let its mournful echoes roll
From sphere to sphere, from pole to pole,
O'er the flight of the greatest, kingliest soul
　　That ever in battle fell.

Yes, weep! weep! weep!
　　Weep for the hero fled!
For death, the greatest of soldiers, at last
Has over our leader his black pall cast,
And from us his noble form hath passed
　　To the home of the mighty dead.

Then toll! and weep! and mourn!
　　Mourn the fall of the brave!
For Jackson, whose deeds made the nation proud,
At whose very name the enemy cowed,
With the " crimson cross " for his martial shroud,
　　Now sleeps his long sleep in the grave.

His form has passed away;
   His voice is silent and still;
No more at the head of " the old brigade,"
The daring men who were never dismayed,
Will he lead them to glory that never can fade —
   Stonewall of the Iron Will!

He fell as a hero should fall;
   'Mid the thunder of war he died.
While the rifle cracked and the cannon roared,
And the blood of the friend and foeman poured,
He dropped from his nerveless grasp the sword
   That erst was the nation's pride.

Virginia, his mother, is bowed;
   Her tread is heavy and slow.
From all the South comes a wailing moan,
And mountains and valleys reëcho the groan,
For the gallant chief of her clans has flown,
   And a nation is filled with woe.

Rest, warrior! rest!
   Rest in thy laurelled tomb!
Thy mem'ry shall live through all of earth's years,
And thy name still excite the despot's fears,
While o'er thee shall fall a nation's tears;
   Thy deeds shall not perish in gloom.

REBELS.

" General Beauregard, now in command of the Rebel
forces in Charleston, has much fame as a tactician." —
Harpers' Weekly.

YES, call them Rebels ! 't is the name
    Their patriot fathers bore,
And by such deeds they 'll hallow it,
    As they have done before.
At Lexington, and Baltimore,
    Was poured the holy chrism,
For Freedom marks her sons with blood,
    In sign of their baptism.

Rebels, in proud and bold protest,
    Against a power unreal ;
A unity which every quest
    Proves false as 't is ideal.
A brotherhood, whose ties are chains,
    Which crushes what it holds,
Like the old marble Laocoön
    Beneath its serpent folds.

Rebels against the malice vast,
    Malice, that nought disarms,

Which fills the quiet of their homes
　　With vague and dread alarms.
Against the invaders' daring feet,
　　Against the tide of wrong,
Which has been borne, in silence borne,
　　But borne perchance too long.

They would be cowards, did they crouch
　　Beneath the lifted hand,
Whose very wave, ye seem to think,
　　Will chill them where they stand.
Yes, call them Rebels ! 't is a name
　　Which speaks of other days,
Of gallant deeds, and gallant men,
　　And wins them to their ways.

Fair was the edifice they raised,
　　Uplifting to the skies ;
A mighty Samson 'neath its dome
　　In grand quiescence lies.
Dare not to touch his noble limb,
　　With thong or chain to bind,
Lest ruin crush both you and him,—
　　This Samson is not blind !

SEVENTY-SIX AND SIXTY-ONE. .

BY JOHN W. OVERALL.

YE spirits of the glorious dead !
  Ye watchers in the sky !
Who sought the patriot's crimson bed,
  With holy trust and high —
Come, lend your inspiration now,
  Come fire each Southern son,
Who nobly fights for freemen's rights,
  And shouts for sixty-one.

Come, teach them how on hill, on glade,
  Quick leaping from your side,
The lightning flash of sabres made
  A red and flowing tide ;
How well ye fought, how bravely fell,
  Beneath our burning sun,
And let the lyre, in strains of fire,
  So speak of sixty-one.

There 's many a grave in all the land,
  And many a crucifix,
Which tells how that heroic band
  Stood firm in seventy-six —

Ye heroes of the deathless past,
　Your glorious race is run,
But from your dust springs freemen's trust,
　And blows for sixty-one.

We build our altars where you lie,
　On many a verdant sod,
With sabres pointing to the sky,
　And sanctified of God;
The smoke shall rise from every pile,
　Till Freedom's cause is won,
And every mouth throughout the South
　Shall shout for sixty-one!

———◆———

KENTUCKY.

BY ESTELLE.

" Just send for us Kentucky boys,
　And we 'll protect you, ladies." — *Old Song.*

THEN, leave us not, Kentucky boys,
　Though thick upon thy border,
The vulture flaps his restless wing,
　And scowls the dark marauder.

Kentucky blood is just as proud,
  Kentucky powder ready,
Kentucky hearts are just as brave,
  Kentucky nerve as steady,

As when the flag we once revered,
  Unfolded o'er her proudly,
And for the South, Kentucky's voice,
  Undaunted, echoed loudly.

The lion-hearted hero then,
  Who led that gallant number,
Must surely feel a sad unrest
  Disturb his death-cold slumber.

And one whose sire, on history's page,
  Is blent in proudest story,
Fell on a Southern field, and bathed
  His dying brow in glory.

Fell, overcome by savage foes,
  Yet still their rage defying;
" *These*, give my father," cried the son,
  " And tell him how I 'm dying."

But now that flag is vilely stained,
  Its sacred rights invaded —

Wrong and dishonor wield the staff;
  Its glory 's sadly shaded.

And when we would its dying spark
  Snatch from the blackening ashes,
And worship once again its light,
  As through the world it flashes,

Kentucky leans upon her arms,
  And coldly looks about her,
Till hirelings, at her very door,
  Dare threaten, and to flout her.

Desert us now, Kentucky boys,
  And on the future dawning,
Thy faded glory scarce will streak
  The first gray light of morning.

Heed not the starveling crew, who hang
  Upon the blue Ohio,
A craven heart each traitor bears,
  And dare not venture nigher.

And should they — know ye not the blood
  Within our full hearts beaming ? —
At once ten thousand scabbards fly,
  Ten thousand blades are gleaming !

Then, waken from thy nerveless sleep,
  Gird on thy well-tried armor,
And soon the braggart North will feel,
  That Right has strength to harm her.

Kentucky boys and girls have we —
  From us ye may not take them;
Sad hearted will ye give them up,
  And for the foe forsake them?

Oh, Tennessee, twin-sister, grieves,
  To take thy hand at parting,
And feel that from its farewell grasp
  A brother's blood is starting.

It must not be! Kentucky, come!
  Virginia loudly calls thee;
And Maryland defenceless stands,
  To share what fate befalls thee.

Come ere the tyrant's chain is forged,
  From out the war-cloud looming;
Come ere thy palsied knee is bent,
  To hopeless ruin dooming.

VIRGINIA'S MESSAGE TO THE SOUTHERN STATES.

YOU dared not think I 'd *never* come,
  You could not doubt your Mother ;
If traitorous chains had crushed my *form*,
  My *soul* with yours had hovered.
Yes, children, *I have come ;*
We 'll stand together, we 'll be one,
Brave dangers, death, and wars begun !

Where should this struggle work and end ?
  Where should this conflict be ?
Where should we all our rights defend,
  And gain our liberty ?
Upon *my* soil your swords you 'll wield,
Upon *my* soil your homes you 'll shield,
And on *my* soil your foes *shall* yield !

Where, but on *my* mountain's heights,
  And on *my* rivers' banks,
Where, but 'neath *my* heavens' lights,
  And in *my* children's camps,
Shall all the blood be shed,
In streams of living red,
And all our foes be dead ?

Upon this earth is there a spot,
  So fit to give a battle-field ?
In all the country, *there is not*,
  Nor one so brave to shield.
If you doubt it, scorn history's pages,
If you doubt it, *mark other ages*,
And come together for the war that rages.

Then, soldiers brave, come forth,
  You sons of *noble mothers !*
They 'll chide you if you 're loath,
  And yield your homes to others.
Mothers ! send them, then, without a tear,
Bid them go, and make all earth revere
Their country's honor and a soldier's bier !

———◆———

A POEM WHICH NEEDS NO DEDICATION.

BY JAMES BARRON HOPE.

WHAT ! you hold yourselves as freemen ?
  Tyrants love just such as ye !
Go ! abate your lofty manner !
Write upon the State's old banner,
  "A furore Normanorum,
  Libera nos, O Domine ! "

Sink before the Federal altars,
   Each one, low on bended knee;
Pray, with lips that sob and falter,
This prayer from a coward's Psalter:
   "A furore Normanorum,
   Libera nos, O Domine!"

But you hold that quick repentance
   In the Northern mind will be;
This repentance comes no sooner
Than the robber's did at Luna.*
   "A furore Normanorum,
   Libera nos, O Domine!"

He repented him; the Bishop
   Gave him absolution free —
Poured upon him sacred chrism
In the pomp of his baptism
   " A furore Normanorum,
   Libera nos, O Domine! "

He repented; then, he sickened —
   Was he pining for the sea?

* The incident with which I have illustrated my opinion of the policy of those who would have us wait for a "reaction at the North," may be found in *Milman's Latin Christianity*, vol. iii. p. 133.

In extremis he was shriven,
The Viaticum was given;
  " A furore Normanorum,
  Libera nos, O Domine ! "

Then, the old cathedral's choir
  Took the plaintive minor key,
With the Host upraised before him,
Down the marble aisle they bore him.
  " A furore Normanorum,
  Libera nos, O Domine ! "

And the Bishop, and the Abbot,
  And the monks of high degree,
Chanting praise to the Madonna,
Came to do him Christian honor.
  " A furore Normanorum,
  Libera nos, O Domine ! "

Now, the Miserere's cadence
  Takes the voices of the sea; —
As the music-billows quiver
See the dead freebooter shiver !
  " A furore Normanorum,
  Libera nos, O Domine ! "

Is it that those intonations
  Thrill him thus from head to knee ?

So ! his cerements burst asunder !
'T is a sight of fear and wonder !
  " A furore Normanorum,
  Libera nos, O Domine ! "

Fierce he stands before the Bishop —
  Dark as shape of Destinie !
Hark ! a shriek ascends, appalling !
Down the prelate goes, dead — falling ;
  " A furore Normanorum,
  Libera nos, O Domine ! "

HASTING lives !　He was but feigning !
  What !　Repentant ?　Never he !
Down he smites the priests and friars,
And the city lights with fires.
  " A furore Normanorum,
  Libera nos, O Domine ! "

Ah ! the children and the maidens,
  'T is in vain they strive to flee !
Where the white-haired priests lie bleeding
Is no place for tearful pleading.
  " A furore Normanorum,
  Libera nos, O Domine ! "

Louder swells the frightful tumult ;
  Pallid Death holds reverie ;

Dies the organ's mighty clamor,
By the Norseman's iron hammer.
   "A furore Normanorum,
   Libera nos, O Domine!"

And they thought that he repented!
   Had they nailed him to a tree,
He had not deserved their pity,
And — they had not lost their city.
   " A furore Normanorum,
   Libera nos, O Domine!"

There 's a moral in this story,
   Which is plain as truth can be :
If we trust the North's relenting,
We will shriek, too late, repenting,
   " A furore Normanorum,
   Libera nos, O Domine!"

—◆—

WILL YOU GO?

BY ESTELLE.

WILL you go? will you go?
   Where the foeman's steel is bright,
In the thickest of the fight,
   For God and for right.
   Will you go? will you go?

Will you stay ? will you stay ?
And let eternal blame
Mark with finger-point of shame
Your deep dishonored name.
Will you stay ? will you stay ?

Will you go ? will you go ?
For Freedom's struggling cry
In the name of God most high,
To rescue her or die.
Will you go ? will you go ?

Will you stay ? will you stay ?
While the coil is tighter bound,
And the tyrant on our ground
Plants his foot with dismal sound.
Will you stay ? will you stay ?

Will you go ? will you go ?
Where our dying brothers' call,
As they bleed and bravely fall,
To free us from this thrall.
Will you go ? will you go ?

Will you stay ? will you stay ?
And let the silent grave
Reproach you for the brave

Who have died our land to save.
   Will you stay ? will you stay ?

Will you go ? will you go ?
The brow of boyhood bared,
With the old and hoary-haired
Have the darkest perils dared.
   Will you go ? will you go ?

Will you stay ? will you stay ?
Slaves of a tyrant's chain,
Slaves ever to remain,
In dishonor's deepest stain.
   Will you stay ? will you stay ?

Will you go ? will you go ?
Answer YES, or answer No,
For soon the fatal blow
Will descend for weal or woe.
   Will you go ? will you go ?

Will you stay ? will you stay ?
Then may eternal gloom,
Draped by the hand of doom,
Forever shroud your tomb.
   CAN you stay ? CAN you stay ?

GOD SAVE THE SOUTH.

GOD bless our Southern land!
   Guard our beloved land!
      God save the South!
Make us victorious,
Happy and glorious;
Spread thy shield over us;
      God save the South!

God of our sires, arise!
Scatter our enemies,
      Who mock Thy truth;
Confound their politics,
Frustrate their knavish tricks:
In Thee our faith we fix;
      God save the South!

In the fierce battle-hour,
With Thine almighty power,
      Assist our youth;
May they, with victory crowned,
Joining our choral round,
With heart and voice resound,
      " God save the South! "

THE BATTLE OF THE MISSISSIPPI.

THE tyrant's broad pennant is floating
  In the South, o'er our waters so blue ;
On our homes now his foul eye is gloating ; —
  The homes of the brave and the true.
    But our flag at the " head of the Passes,"
      Is borne by men brave and true ;
      We will teach them to fear our " Manassas; "
        Three cheers for OUR Red, White, and Blue

We will give his proud fleet such a greeting
  As the storm-cloud's shaft to the tree ;
As the rock to the wave in their meeting —
  Is the stroke of the brave and the free.

Though his minions may come as the locust,
  And outnumber the sands of the sea,
Their numbers will serve to provoke us
  To dare, to die, or live free.

Every breeze from the " Crescent " is laden
  With defiance to the despot on our shore ;
Strong men, the child, and each maiden
  Join in chorus with the cannon's loud roar.

        * The Rebel Ram.

And our flag at the " head of the Passes "
  Is borne by men brave and true ;
We will teach them to fear *our* " Manassas ; "
  Three cheers for OUR Red, White and Blue.

———◆———

ON! SOUTHRON, ON!

ON! Southron on !
    Your flag 's unfurled
'Mid clashing steel, and death-shot hurled,
And war's dark storm-cloud, swiftly whirled,
    Your country calls.   On ! Southron, on !

Strike ! Southron, strike !
The foeman's trail
    Is marked with blood and flame alike ;
And woman's shriek, and infant's wail,
Show that he wars upon the frail
    A war of hate.   Strike ! Southron, strike !

Can manhood fly,
And, recreant, brave
    The silent scorn, the averted eye, —
Decked in its chains, — a cringing slave ?
No ! rather seek a soldier's grave,
    And show the tyrant how to die.

Then, Southron, on !
By all that 's dear,
    By feeble age, and childhood's dawn,
By mother's love, and maiden's prayer,
The brother's blood, the sister's tear, —
    One glance to Heaven, then, Southron, on !

W. B. L.

CIVILE BELLUM.

"In this fearful struggle between North and South,
there are hundreds of cases in which fathers are arrayed
against sons, brothers against brothers." — *American
paper*.

RIFLEMAN, shoot me a fancy shot,
    Straight at the heart of yon prowling vidette ;
Ring me a ball on the glittering spot,
    That shines on his breast like an amulet ! "

" Ah ! Captain, here goes for a fine-drawn bead ;
    There 's music around, when my barrel 's in
        tune."
Crack ! went the rifle ; the messenger sped,
    And dead from his horse fell the ringing dragoon.

" Now, rifleman, steal through the bushes and
        snatch
    From your victim, some trinket to handsel first
        blood ;
A button, a loop, or that luminous patch,
    That gleams in the moon like a diamond-stud."

" O Captain ! I staggered and sunk in my track,
    When I gazed on the face of the fallen vidette;
For he looked so like you as he lay on his back,
    That my heart rose upon me and masters me
        yet.

" But I snatched off the trinket — this locket of
        gold —
    An inch from the centre my lead broke its way,
Scarce grazing the picture, so fair to behold,
    Of a beautiful lady in bridal array."

" Ha ! rifleman, fling me the locket — 't is she :
    My brother's young bride — and the fallen
        dragoon
Was her husband — hush ! soldier, 't was heaven's
        decree ;
    We must bury him there by the light of the
        moon !

"But hark! the far bugles their warning unite;
  War is a virtue — weakness a sin;
There 's a lurking and loping around us to-night;
  Load again, rifleman, keep your hand in!

FROM THE ONCE UNITED STATES.

London Once a Week.

WAR SONG.

COME! come! come!
  Come, brothers, you are called;
Come, each one, unappalled;
  Come, and defend your home!

Come! come! come!
Your doom you now may seal,
If vain be this appeal;
  Come, men, defend your home!

Come! come! come!
Your foes I see afar;
They hate each Southern star;
  Come, men, defend your home!

Come! come! come!
The cannon's belching roar,
The musket's deadly pour
  Cry, men, defend your home!

Come! come! come!
Tread as your fathers trod,
While trusting in their God
  And fighting for their home!

Come! come! come!
Let the invitation sound,
Through town and country round,
  Come, men, defend your home!

Come! come! come!
Ring it through forest wild,
Rouse up each Southern child,
  To wake, and fight for home!

Come! come! come!
The murdered blood of those
Struck down by cruel foes,
  Cries, men, defend your home!

Come! come! come!
Their helpless ones oppressed,

Consider those most blessed,
  Who can defend their home!

Come! come! come!
Oh! ere the foes you hate,
Shall rivet fast your fate,
  Come, men, defend your home!

Come! come! come!
Now, with hearts and hands united,
May your foes soon be requited,
  By men fighting for their home!

Come! come! come!
With a prayer to Him on high;
God grant us victory,
  While fighting for our home!

Come! come! come!
Wait not, lest you live to see
Your loved ones crushed by tyranny,
  And desolate your home!

"FOLLOW, BOYS! FOLLOW!"

BY MILLIE MAYFIELD.

FOLLOW, brave boys, follow !
  'T is the roll-call of the drum,
And the bright steel's ringing music,
  With its spirit-stirring hum —
'T is the tramp of arméd columns,
  Brazen fronted, drawing near,
And the rattle of the sabres
  In the scabbards, that ye hear ; —
    Follow, follow, 't is the van, boys,
      So bravely leading on ;
    Follow, follow, to a man, boys,
      There 's glory to be won !

Follow, follow, saith the mother —
  Follow, follow, saith the wife —
Though ye 're dear as our hearts' blood,
  More precious, far, than life ;
But we would not have ye linger
  While the hated foeman stands
Beside our sacred hearth-stones,
  And desecrates our lands !

We 'll forgive the starting tear, boys,
'T is the jewel of the heart,
That we may not blush to wear, boys,
When from loved ones thus ye part.

There 's not a Southern matron
But in her bosom wears
The iron Key of Firmness
That locketh up her fears ;
While ye buckle on your armor,
She will bid ye safe " God-speed,"
And bear her cross all bravely
For her precious country's need !
When our women have such souls, boys,
Ye must never flinch or quail —
While the storm of battle rolls, boys,
Ne'er strike the straining sail !

Our lives are dearly purchased,
When bondage is the price ;
And what is home, where freedom
Withers 'neath the tyrant's vice ?
Better the earthy pillow,
Better the gory bier,
Where the true-hearted ever
Will drop the burning tear ;

For think, if ye should fall, boys,
   Ye have not lived in vain —
On the brave soldier's pall, boys,
   None ever put a stain !

Fling out our glorious banner
   Upon the golden air —
Swear by its stars, Dishonor
   Shall leave no footprint there !
That ye 'll plant its broad bars firmly,
   As a barrier to the foe,
From the blue Gulf to the Border,
   From the Sea to Mexico !
     The Southern sky 's a-flame, boys,
       Where our stately cities burn,
     But, as monuments of fame, boys,
       Their ashes we 'll in-urn !

Oh ! inch by inch, repel him,
   The foul invading foe !
Let the sharp sabre tell him
   How despots are laid low !
And history's burning pencil
   Will, on her golden page,
Your hero name enamel
   An honor to the age !

> One blow, and we are free boys,
>> Strike firmly, and 't is done !
> On, on, to Tennessee, boys,
>> Oh ! follow bravely on !

BOMBARDMENT OF VICKSBURGH.

DEDICATED WITH RESPECT AND ADMIRATION TO MAJOR-GENERAL
EARL VAN DORN.

FOR sixty days and upwards
>> A storm of shell and shot
Rained round as in a flaming shower,
>> But still we faltered not !
" If the noble city perish,"
>> Our grand young leader said,
" Let the only walls the foe shall scale
>> Be ramparts of the dead !"

For sixty days and upwards
>> The eye of heaven waxed dim,
And even throughout God's holy morn,
>> O'er Christian's prayer and hymn,
Arose a hissing tumult,
>> As if the fiends of air
Strove to engulf the voice of faith
>> In the shrieks of their despair.

There was wailing in the houses,
   There was trembling on the marts,
While the tempest raged and thundered,
   'Mid the silent thrill of hearts ;
But the Lord, our shield, was with us,
   And ere a month had sped,
Our very women walked the streets,
   With scarce one throb of dread.

And the little children gambolled —
   Their faces purely raised,
Just for a wondering moment,
   As the huge bombs whirled and blazed !
Then turning with silvery laughter
   To the sports which children love,
Thrice mailed in the sweet, instinctive thought,
   That the good God watched above.*

Yet the hailing bolts fell faster
   From scores of flame-clad ships,

---

* It has been stated by one professing to have witnessed the fact, that some weeks after the beginning of this terrific bombardment, not only were ladies seen coolly walking the streets, but that in some parts of the town, children were observed at play, only interrupting their sports to gaze and listen at the bursting shells.

And above us denser, darker,
   Grew the conflict's wild eclipse,
Till a solid cloud closed o'er us,
   Like a type of doom and ire,
Whence shot a thousand quivering tongues
 · Of forked and vengeful fire.

But the unseen hands of angels
   These death-shafts warned aside,
And the dove of heavenly mercy
   Ruled o'er the battle tide;
In the houses ceased the wailing,
   And through the war-scarred marts
The people strode with the step of hope
   To the music in their hearts.

COLUMBIA, S. C., *August* 6, 1862.

----♦----

LINES WRITTEN IN FORT WARREN.

BY A CAPTIVE.

SEE ye not that the day is breaking —
   Freemen from their slumbers waking —
Mightier efforts daily making
      To break the oppressor's chain ?

Who would bow to Northern power ?
Who would quail in this stern hour ?
Who, when clouds of darkness lower,
    Could tamely yield again ?

Freemen, to the tented field !
Right and Justice be your shield ;
Make the cruel foeman yield
    Your rights and liberty !

Strike — as ye have struck before !
Strike — as ye have struck, once more !
Strike — as patriot sires of yore,
    Determined to be free !

Strike the vile usurper low !
Strike with Freedom's hand the blow !
Teach the proud, insulting foe
    What freemen feel and dare.

Day is breaking in the West,
O'er the land that I love best,
Patriot fires in every breast,
    God and Liberty are there !

" THE YANKEE DEVIL."

BY W. P. RIVERS.

The " Nondescript,"or "Yankee Devil," for clearing the harbor, was washed ashore on yesterday at Morris Island, and is now in our possession. It is described as an old scow-like vessel, painted red, with a long protruding beak, and jutting iron prongs and claws, intended for the removal of torpedoes. It was attached to the Passaic, and managed by her during the engagement.—*Charleston Courier.*

The enemy are waiting for a new machine, (" Devil,") to remove the torpedoes in the harbor, and to have everything in readiness before the attack. — *Same paper.*

HURRAH! hurrah! good news and true,
    Our woes will soon be past;
To Charleston, boys, all praise be due,
    The devil 's caught at last. .

He 's caught, he 's dead, and met his fate
    On Morris Island's sands ;
His carcass lies in solemn state,
    The spoil of Rebel hands.

Hurrah ! hurrah ! let Dixie cheer !
What may not Charleston do !

The devil's caught at last, we hear;
  A Yankee devil, too!

The blackest, bluest from below,
  The prince of all is he,
Who leads the Yankees where they go,
  On land, or on the sea.

The news is true, all doubt dispel,
  All grief and fears be o'er!
The chiefest from perdition's well
  Lies on a Southern shore.

On South Carolina's beach he lies, —
  His majesty ashore!
Ah! well we know that devil dies
  Who enters at that door.

His name and hue, and shape and size,
  Identify the beast;
'T is he — the father of all lies,
  Of devils not the least.

Scow-like across the deep he came,
  Blood-red his iron sides;
With beak, and claws, and fins of flame
  To plough the vernal tides.

Like serpents which Minerva sent
    To crush the Trojan sire,
So Northern devils come to vent
    On Charleston blood and fire.

But Neptune ne'er decreed the fate
    Of Laocoön's dear sons,
To gratify the Yankees' hate
    On Charleston's dearer ones.

They 'll never bear one fatal hour
    The Northern serpent's coil,
Nor feel the Yankee devil's power
    Who come to crush and spoil.

The " Nondescript," name chosen well;
    The " Northern Devil," aye !
A fiend, a ghoul, a spirit fell !
    Who may describe it — say ?

Foul, artful, bloody, false, insane,
    This Northern ghote* of sin ;
The heathen hells could ne'er contain
    A darker power within.

* Ghote — an imaginary evil being among Eastern nations.

But now, hurrah, the devil 's dead !
  High, dry upon the shore !
Rebellion still may rear its head,
  The war will soon be o'er.

Hold, not so fast, abate your cheer,
  The battle is not won ;
Another devil comes, we hear,
  Before the work is done.

Alas ! when will this warfare end ?
  Not till all Yankee foes are dead ;
For nondescript is each — or fiend —
  His soul with murder red.

Cave Spring, Ga., *April* 11, 1863.

LINES TO THE SOUTHERN BANNER.

DEAR flag ! that wooes the morning air,
  That floats upon the midnight breeze
Victorious on the battle-field,
  Victorious on the seas —
We bless thee as we see thee gleam
In glory o'er each Southern plain.

Dark was the hour when first thy folds
   Were given to the wind —
And sable clouds from Northern skies
   Did fiercely o'er thee bend —
But still thy stars with lustre shone,
   Despite the North-cloud's low'ring gloom.

At Sumter soon in glory thou
   Didst o'er thy haughty rival ride,
There shame didst stamp on vandal brow
   There first didst blast the vandal pride,
And gave the vandal horde to know
" At least thou wert a worthy foe ! "

Then thou didst kiss Virginia's sky,
   Didst gild Manassas with thy beams,
And force the dastard foe to fly
   Back from our sunny plains,
Unable to endure thy light,
Or to resist the Southron's might.

Nor is it on the land alone
   That thou dost emblem victory;
But where the eternal billows roam
   Thou hast looked down with eagle eye
On contests where the Northern foe
Before the Southron's arm bent low.

Full brightly gleam thy noble bars,
  Thy stars in radiant circle shine,
Emblem of the eternity
  Of our young Southron clime,
The lost Atlantis poets sung,
Which has amid the nations sprung.

Loved flag! mayst thou forever float
  Above this fairest of earth's realms,
And mayst thou neighboring nations take
  " Beneath the shadow of thy wings ; "
May Mexico and the Indian isles
Soon bask beneath thy loving smiles.

Forever untarnished be thy folds,
  Forever increasing be thy stars,
And in the realms thou floatest o'er,
  Be naught of strife, be naught that mars ;
And mayst thou be the last to shine,
When Heaven proclaims the end of time.

THE BOY-SOLDIER.

BY A LADY OF SAVANNAH.

HE is acting o'er the battle,
　　With his cap and feather gay,
Singing out his soldier prattle,
　　In a mockish, manly way —
With the boldest, bravest footstep,
　　Treading firmly up and down,
And his banner waving softly
　　O'er his boyish locks of brown.

And I sit beside him sewing,
　　With a busy heart and hand,
For the gallant soldiers going
　　To the far-off battle-land ;
And I gaze upon my jewel,
　　In his baby-spirit bold,
My little blue-eyed soldier,
　　Just a second summer old.

Still a deep, deep well of feeling,
　　In my mother's heart is stirred,
And the tears come softly stealing
　　At each imitative word.

There 's a struggle in my bosom,
  For I love my darling boy —
He 's the gladness of my spirit,
  He 's the sunlight of my joy !
Yet I think upon my country,
  And my spirit groweth bold,
Oh ! I wish my blue-eyed soldier
  Were but twenty summers old !

I would speed him to the battle,
  I would arm him for the fight,
I would give him to his country,
  For his country's wrong and right !
I would nerve his hand with blessing,
  From the " God of Battles " won ;
With *His* helmet and *His* armor,
  I would cover o'er my son.

Oh ! I *know* there 'd be a struggle,
  For I love my darling boy ;
He 's the gladness of my spirit,
  He 's the sunlight of my joy !
Yet in thinking on my country,
  Oh ! my spirit groweth bold ;
And I wish my blue-eyed soldier
  Were but twenty summers old.

THE VIRGINIANS OF THE VALLEY.

BY FRANK TICKNOR, M. D.

Sic Jurat.

THE knightliest of the knightly race,
  Who, since the days of old,
Have kept the lamp of chivalry
  Alight in hearts of gold;
The kindliest of the kindly band
  Who rarely hated ease,
Who rode with Smith around the land
  And Raleigh round the seas!

Who climbed the blue Virginia hills,
  Amid embattled foes,
And planted there in valleys fair,
  The lily and the rose;
Whose fragrance lives in many lands,
  Whose beauty stars the earth,
And lights the hearths of many homes
  With loveliness and worth!

We thought they slept! the sons who kept
  The names of noble sires,
And slumbered while the darkness crept
  Around their vigil fires!

But still the Golden Horse-shoe knights,
  Their Old Dominion keep,
Whose foes have found enchanted ground,
  But not a knight asleep.
     Torch Hall, Ga.

THE SWEET SOUTH.

BY W. GILMORE SIMMS.

O THE sweet South! the sunny, sunny South!
  Land of true feeling, land forever mine!
I drink the kisses of her rosy mouth,
  And my heart swells as with a draught of wine;
She brings me blessings of maternal love;
  I have her smile which hallows all my toil;
Her voice persuades, her generous smiles approve,
  She sings me from the sky and from the soil!
O, by her lonely pines that wave and sigh!
  O, by her myriad flowers, that bloom and fade,
By all the thousand beauties of her sky,
  And the sweet solace of her forest shade,
    She 's mine — she 's ever mine —
    Nor will I aught resign

Of what she gives me, mortal or divine;
    Will sooner part
    With life, hope, heart, —
Will die — before I fly!

O, love is hers, — such love as ever glows
    In souls where leap affections living tide;
She is all fondness to her friends; to foes
    She glows a thing of passion, strength, and pride;
She feels no tremors when the danger 's nigh,
    But the fight over and the victory won,
How with strange fondness, turns her loving eye
    In tearful welcome on each gallant son!
O! by her virtues of the cherished past, —
    By all her hopes of what the future brings, —
I glory that my lot with her is cast,
    And my soul flushes and exulting sings;
        She 's mine — she 's ever mine —
        For her will I resign
All precious things — all placed upon her shrine;
    Will freely part
    With life, hope, heart —
Will die — do aught but fly!

THE SOUTHERN CROSS.*

IN the name of God! Amen!
  Stand for our Southern rights!
Arm ye Southern men,
  The God of Battle fights!
Fling the invaders far,
  Hurl back their work of woe
The voice is the voice of a brother,
  But the hands are the hands of a foe.
They come with a trampling army,
  Invading our native sod —
Stand, Southrons! fight and conquer!
  In the name of the Mighty God!

They're singing our song of triumph,
  Which was made to make us free,
While they're breaking away the heartstrings
  Of our nation's harmony.
Sadly it floateth from us,
  Sighing o'er land and wave,
Till mute on the lips of the poet,
  It sleeps in his Southern grave.

* To His Excellency President Davis, from his fellow-citizens, Ellen Key Blunt, J. T. Mayson Blunt, of Maryland and Virginia.

Spirit and song departed !
  Minstrel and minstrelsy !
We mourn thee, heavy-hearted,
  But we will, we shall be free !

They are waving our flag above us,
  With a despot's tyrant will ;
With our blood they have stained its colors,
  And call it holy still.
With tearful eyes, but steady hand,
  We 'll tear its stripes apart,
And fling them like broken fetters,
  That may not bind the heart ;
But we 'll save our stars of glory,
  In the might of the sacred sign
Of Him who has fixed forever
  Our Southern Cross to shine.

Stand, Southrons ! stand and conquer !
  Solemn and strong and sure !
The strife shall not be longer
  Than God shall bid endure.
By the life which only yesterday
  Came with the infant's breath,
By the feet which ere the morn may
  Tread to the soldier's death !

By the blood which cries to Heaven !
   Crimson upon our sod !
Stand, Southrons ! stand and conquer !
   In the name of the Mighty God !
      PARIS, 1862.

--- ◆ ---

PATRIOTISM.

THE holy fire that nerved the Greek
   To make his stand at Marathon,
Until the last red foeman's shriek
   Proclaimed that Freedom's fight was won,
Still lives unquenched — unquenchable !
   Through every age its fires will burn —
Lives in the hermit's lonely cell,
   And springs from every storied urn !

The hearthstone embers hold the spark
   Where fell Oppression's foot hath trod ;
Through Superstition's shadow dark
   It flashes to the living God !
From Moscow's ashes spring the Russ ;
   In Warsaw Poland lives again ;
Schamyl, on frosty Caucasus,
   Strikes Liberty's electric chain !

Tell's freedom-beacon lights the Swiss;
    Vainly the invader ever strives;
He finds " Sic Semper Tyrannis "
    In San Jacinto's bowie-knives !
Than these — than all — a holier fire
    Now burns thy soul, Virginia's son !
Strike then for wife, babe, gray-haired sire;
    Strike for the grave of Washington !

The Northern rabble aims for greed;
    The hireling parson goads the train —
In that foul crop from bigot seed,
    Old " Praise God Barebones " howls again !
We welcome them to " Southern lands " —
    We welcome them to " Southern slaves " —
We welcome them " with bloody hands
    To hospitable Southern graves ! "

SONG FOR THE MARYLAND LINE.

BY old Potomac's rushing tide
    Our bayonets are gleaming;
And o'er the bounding waters wide
    We gaze while tears are streaming.

The distant hills of Maryland
   Rise sadly up before us,
And tyrant bands have chained our land, —
   Our mother, proud, that bore us.

Our proud old mother's queenly head
   Is bowed in subjugation;
With her children's blood her soil is red,
   And fiends in exultation
Taunt her with shame as they bind her chains,
   While her heart is torn with anguish;
Old mother, on famed Manassas's plains
   Our vengeance did not languish!

We thought of your wrongs as on we rushed,
   'Mid shot and shell appalling;
We heard your voice as it upward gushed
   From the Maryland life-blood falling.
No pity we knew! Did they mercy show
   When they bound the mother that bore us?
But we scattered death 'mid the dastard foe,
   Till they, shrieking, fled before us!

We mourn for our brothers, brave, that fell
   On that field, so stern and gory;
But their spirits rose with our triumph-yell
   To the heavenly realms of glory.

And their bodies rest on the hard won field —
  By their love so true and tender;
We 'll keep the prize they would not yield,
  We 'll die, but we 'll not surrender.

And, mother, we wait but the signal-blast,
  To rush to redeem thy glory;
We may fall, but our conquering dust shall
    rest
  On thy soil, so famed in story.
The tyrant's flag shall no longer shine,
  Thy liberty to smother,
When the word is passed to the Maryland
    Line,
  To strike for their loved old mother.

—◆—

THE SOUTH FOR ME.

THE South for me ! the sunny clime,
  Where earth is clothed in beauty's hue,
And Nature vies in scenes sublime,
  With all the Old World ever knew;
I love thy soil where'er I roam,
  Sweet land ! and when afar from thee,
My fond heart throbs with thoughts of home,
  And echoes back " the South for me."

Chorus — The South for me, the South for me,
  The golden clime the heart desires,
  The only land where men are free,
  And worthy of their free-born sires.

The South for me! the patriot's heart
 Beats ever to that slogan-cry;
And heroes, armed and ready, start
 For their loved land, to do or die;
But leave the Southron's valor free,
 Let Southern heroes meet the foe,
And when rings out " the South for me " —
 Their strong right arms will deal the blow.
  The South for me, &c.

The South for me! — its bright-eyed maids,
 Its clime, its stars, its silver skies,
Its streamlets with their lovely naiads,
 Its vales where varying beauties rise,
Its cotton-fields, where dusky slaves,
 Are happy in protection kind, —
The stranger's home, though Yankee knaves
 May never there a welcome find.
  The South for me, &c.

CONFEDERATE LAND.

BY H. H. STRAWBRIDGE.

STATES of the South! Confederate Land!
  Our foe has come — the hour is nigh;
His bale-fires rise on every hand, —
  Rise as one man, to do or die!
From mountain, vale, and prairie wide,
  From forest vast, and field, and glen,
And crowded city, pour thy tide,
  Oh! fervid South! of patriot men.
      Up! old and young; the weak, be strong!
      Rise for the right, — hurl back the wrong,
      And foot to foot, and hand to hand,
      Strike for our own Confederate Land!

Make every house, and rock, and tree,
  And hill, your forts; and fen and flood
Yield not! our soil shall rather be
  One waste of flame, one sea of blood!
Fear not their steel, but fear their gold —
  Not Yankee force, but Yankee fraud;
Trust not the race — as false as cold —
  Whose very prayers are lies to God.
      Up! old and young, &c.

Armed, or unarmed, stand fearless forth,
  Sons of the South ! stand, wife and maid !
Against the foul insidious North,
  Our *babes* shall wield the battle-blade !
On ! though perennial be the strife,
  For honor dear, for hearth-stone fire ;
Give blow for blow ! take life for life !
  " Strike ! till the last armed foe expire ! "
    Up ! old and young, &c.

----◆----

THE SONG OF THE SOUTH.

HURRAH for the South, the glorious South !
    the land of song and story —
Her name shall ring, and the world shall sing her
    honor, fame, and glory ;
For the skies above which smiled in love, are dark
    with hearth-fires burning,
She rises in might to defend the right, on her treach-
    erous brethren turning.
    Sons of the South, arise ! arise !
      For never shall fall upon her —
    The land we love all the earth above —
      One stain of dark dishonor.

Hurrah for the South, the gallant South, with her
      great heart proudly beating:
She takes her stand at Freedom's hand, and dreams
      not of retreating;
Oh! Southern boys, for fireside joys, with their
      hearts so brave and tender,
Will relentlessly fight, and to death's dark night
      alone will they surrender.
      Sons of the South, arise! arise!
        For never shall fall upon her —
      The land we love all earth above —
        One stain of dark dishonor.

No Northern band shall rule this land — to the
      breeze give Freedom's banner,
As its glowing folds o'er our land unroll, from moun-
      tain and savannah;
O'er river and lake the sound shall break, and
      swell with thundering glory;
Hurrah for the South! the noble South! the land
      of war and story!
      Sons of the South, arise! arise!
        For never shall fall upon her —
      The land we love all earth above —
        One stain of dark dishonor.

THE BANNER SONG.

BY JAMES B. MARSHALL.

UP, up with the banner, the foe is before us,
 His bayonets bristle, his sword is unsheathed,
Charge, charge on his line with harmonious chorus,
 For the prayers go with us that beauty has
  breathed.

He fights for the power of despot and plunder,
 While we are defending our altars and homes;
He has riven the firmly-knit Union asunder,
 And to bind it with Tyranny's fetters he comes.
Like the prophet Mokanna, whose veil so resplend-
  ent,
 His monstrous deformity closely concealed,
Duplicity marks Lincoln's course, and dependent
 On falsehood is every fair promise revealed.

When that veil shall be raised, Freedom's last
  feast be taken,
 A banquet to which all his followers will crowd;
Oh, horror of horrors! who can view it unshaken?
 Without sense they will sit all in suppliance
  bowed!

We do not forget that they once were our broth-
　　ers,
　　That we sat in our boyhood around the same
　　　　board,
That our heart's best idolatry blest the same moth-
　　ers,
　　And to the same fathers libations we poured.

We rallied around the same star-spangled stand-
　　ard,
　　When called to the field by the tocsin of war,
But they from our side have unfeelingly wandered,
　　And we strip from our flag every recusant star.
They have forced us to stand by our own Constitu-
　　tion,
　　To defend our lov'd homesteads, our altars and
　　　　fires,
While they tamely submit to a tyrant's pollution,
　　Beneath whose foul tread their own freedom
　　　　expires

Then up with the banner, its broad stripes wide
　　flowing,—
　　' T is the emblem of Liberty — flag of the free ;
Let it wave us to triumph, and every heart glowing,
　　Nerve each arm's bravest blow for its lov'd
　　　　Tennessee.

THE INVOCATION.

GOD bless the land of flowers,
And turn its winter hours
To bright summer time!
Be the brave soldier's friend,
And from dangers defend,
When Northern balls descend
On the Southern line!

Father, we implore Thee,
Let Thy people go free
From their foes once more!
And they will bend the knee,
And Thine the praise shall be,
On sunny land and sea,
As in days of yore!

Lord, bid the carnage cease,
Let the banner of peace
Again be unfurled!
Two nations make from one,
And when the work is done,
Over both reign alone, —
Saviour of the world!

B. W. W.

THE END.